DEEP
FREEZE

THE
ICEDOME

D.S. WEISSMAN

The Icedome
Deep Freeze: Book #3

Written by D.S. Weissman

Copyright © 2017 by Abdo Consulting Group, Inc.

Published by EPIC Press™
PO Box 398166
Minneapolis, MN 55439

Printed in the United States of America.

Cover design by Dorothy Toth
Images for cover art obtained from iStockPhoto.com
Edited by Melanie Austin

LIBRARY OF CONGRESS CATALOGING-IN-PUBLICATION DATA

Names: Weissman, D.S., author.
Title: The icedome / by D.S. Weissman.
Description: Minneapolis, MN : EPIC Press, [2017] | Series: Deep freeze ; book #3
Summary: The survivors have built a sustainable existence on their frozen island. Abe stands as
    chief, and James is his right hand man. Elise and Charlotte form a tribal committee, and the
    new settlement must find what it takes to survive under rules created to keep the peace, at
    any cost.
Identifiers: LCCN 2015959223 | ISBN 9781680760170 (lib. bdg.) |
    ISBN 9781680762839 (ebook)
Subjects: LCSH: Adventure and adventurers—Fiction. | Islands—Fiction. | Interpersonal
    relationships—Fiction. | Survival—Fiction. | Human behavior—Fiction. | Young adult
    fiction.
Classification: DDC [Fic]—dc23
LC record available at http://lccn.loc.gov/2015959223

*To all the readers who have ever wanted
to see their enemies shivering inside
a large dome made of ice*

NOSTALGIA FOR FORGOTTEN THINGS

ELISE

Elise's mom liked to do the bills in the kitchen. She would sit at the table with piles of mail stacked higher than her elbows. Sometimes the papers would slide off the table. Her father would stand at the stove and make chili from a can, stirring the pot and saying it didn't have enough salt. He would add salt, then say it didn't have enough meat. They never had enough meat.

"Go to your room, sweetie," her mother said.

"But I want to stay here," she said.

"Dinner will be ready soon."

"You finish your homework?" her dad asked.

"It's Friday," Elise said.

"It is?" he asked. "Guess we'll have to add some tortilla chips to this thing to celebrate then." Elise loved tortilla chips and chili. The salty crunch helped mask the taste of the regular chili. "Now listen to your mom. We'll call you when dinner's ready."

She stood up and saw her reflection in the window. She tried to ignore it. She was too old for pigtails and she never liked the color pink. Her mom had done her hair and her dad had bought her that shirt almost two years ago. She wore it because it fit. Not much fit her anymore. She had asked her mom when they could get new clothes.

"Now's not a good time, baby."

"When will it be a good time?" Elise asked. "Things are tight."

"Yes," her mom said. "They are." Elise meant her clothes.

She walked to her room dressed in the clothes that didn't fit her figure and the hair that didn't fit her personality. Her mom groaned but tried to cover her mouth. That groan had filled the house for over a year. At night when she thought Elise wasn't listening, her mom would rummage through the bills or the bank statements until that sound forced its way out. Before Elise's dad had found the chili on sale at Costco they had eaten ramen noodles for six weeks straight. Sometimes it had eggs. Sometimes he added mushrooms. Before the ramen they had eaten Spaghetti O's. The chili could at least be mixed with something different. On other nights, Elise stuffed the meat byproduct into a hard taco shell. The night before last she smothered it over some noodles. The half-limp pasta reminded her too much of the Spaghetti O's that she never wanted to eat again. She had stuffed her face with so many bad noodles that even the thought of a decent, firm, properly cooked noodle ruined her appetite.

"You check the gas bill?" Elise's father asked.

"Yes, Don," her mother said.

"I'm just trying to help, Olli," her dad said.

"It would be more helpful if—" the silence hurt Elise more than words. She never closed the door but her parents didn't notice. She would silently listen to their arguments, discussions, and whispers. Sometimes it was easier to play ignorant. Her parents rarely knew what to say to each other; what could they possibly say to her?

"If what?" Don said. "If I got a job? That what you were going to say?"

"No," Olli said.

"You know I'm trying. It's been hard lately. It's been hard on everyone."

"It's been hard on everyone. I didn't mean it."

Don sighed. The scrape of the spoon in the metal pot screeched down the hall, piercing Elise's ears. Her parents didn't mention the sound.

"Did you look at the phone bill?" Don asked.

"I paid the gas bill with the money for the phone bill," Olli said.

"The electric?"

"I paid the electric with the gas money. Then

used the water money for the phone bill and the grocery money for the water bill."

"What's that leave us?"

"We could go back to Spaghetti O's for a bit," Olli said.

"Olli," Don said. "I don't think we'd survive if we had another day of Spaghetti O's, ever." Don slurped when he ate. Elise heard him taste the chili. The sound was louder than the spoon scraping the pot but Elise found it comforting. It reminded her that her father was close. "Chili's done," he said. Elise headed to the kitchen.

"I was just about to call you," Olli said. "How do you always know when dinner's ready?"

"Must be a sixth sense," Don said. "Sit. Eat. Enjoy." He scooped a large spoonful into a bowl and cracked tortilla chips over the top.

"Thank you," she said. Her father kissed the top of her head. She took a spoon from the drawer and dug in. The salty and crunchy chips took away from the flavorless pile of meat but at least it wasn't Spaghetti O's. "Are you eating?"

"We will," her mom said. "You first. You've waited longer." Elise ate slowly and watched her parents ignore the empty bowls in front of them. Her mom stared at the bills and her dad stared at her mom. The room smelled burnt. The kitchen filled with haze.

"Oh shit," Don said. "The chili."

"You forgot to turn off the stove?" Olli asked.

"Not now, Olli."

"For Christ sake, that's an extra day's worth."

"I don't need any more," Elise said. She tried to hand her bowl to her mother.

"That's yours, baby."

"Please? I'm not that hungry. I ate at school."

"We made that for you." Olli's eyes were red and tired. Water sat at the edge of her eyelids. Whatever she tried to hide from Elise was obvious. Her cheeks were flush. She groaned again.

"There's more," Elise said.

"Honey," Don said. "We made that for you and you should finish it."

Elise sat back down at the table and tried to force herself to finish the chili she didn't want, to stomach the flavor she didn't like. When she finished the last spoonful she pushed her bowl away. It rambled in a circle before coming to a rest. Elise was ready to pull out the pigtails and throw the ribbons away with the bowl.

"How much you got left?" Don asked.

"It's all gone," Elise said.

"You want to stay in here?" he asked.

"Can I go to my room?"

Her parents nodded and Elise went back to her room. She pulled out a collection of colored pencils that had been worn almost to the nubs. She pulled a paper out of the stack she had on her desk. One side was already colored. Most of the paper she had she took from school. When she wanted to make the paper last longer, she drew shapes that angled out from the corners to maximize space on the page and the time it took her to fill the paper.

"How much do we have left?" Don asked. He had lowered his voice but it still carried down the cavernous halls.

"We're a few hundred short," Olli said. "If we don't come up with it by tomorrow . . . "

"We can figure it out," he said.

"We have nothing left to leverage."

Elise started to make boxes in the right hand corner of the page. It started with two lines; she used the edges of the paper as the box's other borders. Then she cut the first box in half before cutting the next two boxes in half. Then she checkered the pattern and continued outward. Minutes passed. She ignored her parents' voices that rose when they forgot she was in the other room, and fell when they remembered. It was a bit of a routine. Her mom's voice was more strained when she mentioned numbers. More time passed and the page filled with boxes, some shaded in, others left blank.

"It's time for bed, baby."

"Just a little longer?" Elise asked.

"Not tonight." Her mother picked out Elise's pajamas. They fit worse than her other clothes. Olli helped take out the pigtails. Elise climbed into bed. Olli kissed her on the forehead. "You know we love you, right baby?" Elise nodded her head. "No matter what."

"Promise?" Elise asked.

"Of course, baby. Why?"

"Is it okay if I don't wear pigtails anymore?"

"You don't like them?"

Elise shook her head.

"Oh, baby. Why didn't you say something?"

Elise shrugged.

"Were you afraid you would hurt my feelings?"

Elise turned away and nodded.

"You are such a sweet girl." Her mother pushed the hair from Elise's eyes and kissed her again.

"You are my sweet girl. We will always love you. Sometimes that means making hard choices. But it doesn't change the fact that you love someone."

Olli touched Elise's nose with her finger and smiled. Her eyes filled up with tears again. Elise smiled and pulled the sheets to her neck. Her mother walked to the door and turned off the light. The hallway cast a small light into the edge of Elise's room. Her parents continued to whisper, the words lost on Elise. No matter how awful she felt, the sheets against her skin always reassured her. The muffled voices filtered through the walls. Elise heard the comforting sound of her father slurping the chili and drifted off to sleep.

THE ICEDOME

JAMES

THE BOY RAMMED HIS FIST INTO THE OTHER'S SKULL. THEY rained punches down on each other, connecting blow after blow. Their bones cracked, from their jaws to their noses. Each punch drew an excited scream from the crowd. The Fornlanders surrounded the frozen crater they called the "Icedome." Bars made of ice spread along the top, decorating this palace of death. Blood flew from the boys' mouths, their noses, their eyes, and a drying crimson river ran down one's ear. It stained the ground and spattered the ice-bars. No matter how much blood they spilled, the entire dome was wiped clean by the frost of night, which bleached out the destruction and death in everyone's mind.

"One winner! One Life!" The crowed screamed over again. That was the rule, and on this island you never disobeyed the rules.

Sweat crawled down James's face like a spider and gave James a tingling sensation across his skin. He held onto a blurry memory of what spiders looked like. The more he thought about them the more he mixed them up with lizards, turning the four-legged reptiles into six-legged arachnids, not small enough to be spiders but not long-tailed enough to be lizards. He used to be afraid of spiders. The thought of one running down his face would have sent him screaming into another room with his hands slapping at his cheeks. The thoughts of spiders, no matter how deformed, still made him shiver. It had been over a year since he had seen a spider or a lizard.

A shrill scream pierced the dome's bars. Everyone looked down at the boys who fought. Red soaked their ragged, sparse clothes and bare skin. The crowd wore ample clothing to shield them from the cold. The fighters had their fists, stamina, rage, and will to protect them from freezing. One of the fighters would die, but it wouldn't be because of the frost.

It was trial by the gods. James had read once how gladiators would battle for judgment, believing the gods favored virtuousness. At the time James didn't know what virtue meant or what virtuousness was. Shane had accused Gil of stealing. There was no proof, but the rule was simple: Fornlanders couldn't let an accusation go unresolved. The community couldn't allow the accusation to fester between the two boys, letting the situation escalate.

"All problems escalate if not taken care of imme-diately," Abe had said. "You don't need more proof than the world." The world had turned desolate. It was just a matter of time before the settlement forgot about San Diego completely. It had become a world overtaken by international egos and subse-quent despair.

Shane knew the rule when he challenged Gil. If there was no proof and no chance of reconciliation, then they would wind up in the dome. It had happened a handful of times before. The boys wandered in beneath the ice bars with the eyes of Fornland on them.

The worst fight was the first fight: Wendy against Lily. Lily and Elise were close friends. Elise had been the first person to talk to her when she came to Fornland; Elise was always first to reach out to new kids at the orphanage. Elise watched Lily grow and helped her acclimate—she taught her how to dress well without money and use a tampon without feeling embarrassed. James couldn't remember what the accusation against Wendy had been. It could have been a story concocted by Lily, some lasting grudge that Lily was looking for a chance to end. Rumors about Wendy and Lily both liking Jon Zarabi, who everyone called Zara, filtered through to James. Zara chose Wendy. They were happy together for a few weeks, until Lily's challenge.

Once a rumor howled into the night, it was rarely forgotten.

Wendy and Lily entered the dome. The air was empty that day. No one screamed; blood hadn't been tasted yet. Lily was a half-head taller than Wendy. Wendy had cut her hair the night before. Most people kept their hair as long as they could for an extra layer of warmth in the never-ending cold. James didn't question Wendy's reasons; the rest of the settlement quickly understood too. Her black hair was cropped and patchy. Her skin was dark against the snow. Lily's hair was strawberry and frazzled. She didn't even move her hair from her eyes. Wendy looked like a child next to Lily. *They* are *children*, James thought. The Fornlanders were still children. No matter how long they all spent on the island, James felt they would always be children because they'd never learned how to live like adults. The two girls faced each other.

"We don't let things fester here," Abe said. "That's why the world is how it is. That won't happen to us. We settle things." Everyone nodded in understanding. They had understood the words, the sentiment, James knew, but they didn't understand the consequences. "There can only be one winner. That means only one person walks out of here. One winner. One life!" Abe paused and let the words sink in. "That is how we settle things." He rang the bell. He had taken it from the cruise ship spa before the ship burned.

The sound of Wendy's scream filled James's throat with bile. It sent needles up his spine. He hadn't heard a sound as terrifying and troubled since the first deer he had ever seen gurgle its last breath as wild dogs tore it apart. Wendy jumped, wrapped her legs around Lily, dug her teeth into Lily's neck, and coiled her fingers through Lily's hair. When Lily dropped to the ground, Wendy used Lily's hair like rope, slamming her head into the ice. The reason Wendy had cut her own hair was now obvious. Fornland stayed quiet. James wanted to puke. He could already feel the acidic liquid seeping out of his nose.

Wendy's scream vibrated the bars. A crimson pool flowed from Lily's head. Her hair stuck to her skin. Wendy continued smashing Lily's head against the ground. The bloody pool splashed around the dome. Blood stamped Wendy's face. The thick, watery sound vibrated in James's ears. He couldn't turn away. Lily's eyes were blank where a blue speck of light had been. Wendy's voice broke. Her hands dropped from Lily's hair. Lily's head crashed one last time back into the blood James knew wouldn't be there in the morning. Wendy fell back. The pool expanded, seeping into the frozen ground. Wendy stared at Lily. Elise covered her eyes, unable to watch, unable to scream. The Fornlanders stared at them both. But there was one rule and everyone knew not to disobey the rules—only one could leave. After that first fight, no one used the Icedome to settle old scores anymore.

Now Gil and Shane's fight continued. Exhaustion pulled on their bones and their faces. Beneath the anger James saw desperation. Gil's fists were covered in red. James wasn't sure if the blood was Shane's or Gil's. Shane's fists were black and blue. Another punch caused blood to fly upwards across the bars—through the bars. A spider-crawl of sweat dripped from James's cheek, falling to the ground and mixing with the blood. Fornland cheered. Shane dropped to the floor. The fight ended. Blood continued to fall.

THE IDEA OF
PERFECTION

JAMES

THE COMMUNITY WAS BUILT AND WAS THRIVING. *As much as a bunch of teenagers stranded on a frozen island can thrive*, James thought. Through it all, somehow, Fornland had built a community out of whatever they lifted from the stranded cruise ship. This all happened before Robert tried to make his way for literally greener pastures—anywhere with direct sunlight would have been greener—but no one knew if that existed anymore.

James thought it strange that Robert had spent so much time helping them build a community where they could survive just to leave in search of a beach untouched by snow. Abe was chief now and he told the story of what transpired between him and Robert with such conviction that no one had the stomach to question him. James's head swam with possibilities from the moment Abe had told the story about Robert's betrayal.

Whatever Abe had learned about physics and combustion during the months he spent in the engine room of the ship paid off. He had managed to install geothermal pumps, rigged straight from the hot springs at the base of the volcano that loomed overhead. Even though the island was covered from mountaintop to seashore with snow, the settlement had comfortable heat in the rooms they had built.

Robert was gone now, like the rest of the adults who had abandoned them, another remembered of countless missing people. Worst of all, Robert disappeared the same way James's parents had: without a word to him.

The geothermal heat had been Robert's idea, based upon what he had seen when he ran cruises around Sweden. He had started the project, Abe finished the project, and the rest of the Fornlanders maintained it. Charlotte directed the trenches and connected the pipes they had taken from the ship. Every necessary item was liberated by the Fornlanders and spread throughout the new village to keep the rooms warm, including a greenhouse they fabricated out of portholes and other glass. All they had to do was dig up soil and let it thaw in a variety of planters they made from the sheet pans and cooking pots. Charlotte had masterminded the project. With so much taken from the cruise ship it was amazing Robert thought he had enough of the ship to make it off the island.

The lines dividing boys and girls, young and old didn't matter anymore. They had built a village according to their wants. James knew that what they wanted was warmth and space. At the same time, there were enough kids of a certain age more comfortable in the corral system, where they could huddle together at night and tell stories about what life used to be like. James was pretty sure, though, that after months on the boat and months on the island, the young kids couldn't remember what life before the island had been like. The majority of boys and girls decided they wanted collective rooms to secure themselves away from the wild dogs. James understood the feeling of safety in numbers. The largest bunk accommodated the youngest kids that were more comfortable sleeping together than apart. Everyone else separated into at least groups of two, and at most, groups of six. No one over twelve wanted to be in a group of more than six. It made construction last a little longer but everyone was happy to work. Laziness made lethargy and lethargy made doubters or depressants. It had already happened with Buck and Rudy.

Buck's real name was Brad but no one wanted to call him that because it made him sound pretty. Brad was chubby-cheeked and immature but his size made everyone think he would be the person in charge. He mostly followed Rudy around. Rudy's real name was Rudolpho. No one wanted to call him that either. Rudolpho had always been quiet, but liked. He didn't say much to the crowd, but when he did, people listened.

In the halls of the orphanage, tucked beneath the concrete ceilings and halogen lights, Abe had asked Rudy, "Why don't you talk more?" Rudy shrugged his shoulders and took a bite of one of the many Twinkies he kept under his bed. "You're a funny guy."

"I want to keep it that way," Rudy said. Abe laughed and patted Rudy on the back. Rudy took another bite of his Twinkie. He leaned over and said something to Buck. Buck smiled.

"Why do you eat that shit?" Abe asked.

"Everyone has a vice," Rudy said.

When they got to the island, everyone wanted to make Rudy the doctor and Buck his assistant. It was no surprise why Abe thought Buck would make a good assistant; he was large and could lift anyone who needed help, or keep hold of anyone who didn't want help.

Even though Rudy was quiet, he was very intelligent. James wondered if he kept all the good ideas to himself.

"Rudy should be our doctor," Abe said.

"I don't think picking a doctor should be that easy," Elise said. She had grown in the past few months. James remembered her sitting on the ice complaining about the cold moments before he fell into a hole he had dug. Her face was almost covered by her parka. Now she seemed almost regal in the warmth of the community room, which had been built and marked for the use of the committee, which was made up of Abe, Elise, and Abe's advisors: James, Tic-Tac, Shia, Charlotte, and Sarah. Geoff hated everyone chosen and had demanded to be a part of the committee.

"Stick your head in the hot springs and wait till I make a decision," Abe had said.

Geoff never did.

"It's a shame," James said.

"What is?" Tic-Tac asked.

"Geoff," James said. "He never took Abe up on his offer."

Everyone had laughed. Charlotte gave a reluctant smile. James had learned the different variations of her smiles. When something was really funny she convulsed forward once and covered her mouth, hiding a deep, uncontrollable snort. If it was not funny but people laughed, she twisted the corners of her mouth up but kept her lips flat. If she hated it, she shook her head slowly and turned away. She made the tight-lipped smile then. In the meeting about Rudy and Buck, she often turned away when Abe spoke.

"Rudy shows promise," Abe said.

"No one knows the first thing about being a doctor," Sarah said.

"We took the books from the ship's library," Tic-Tac said. "It's the only hope anyone has."

That was the basis of many of their decisions, and also the problem with many of their decisions.

"Except someone burned those books shortly after we made camp," Elise said. Charlotte nodded. Any knowledge of any trade would need to be a combination of previous information and trial by error. Choosing a doctor scared the shit out of James.

Teagan had become their butcher because he volunteered.

"I don't mind animals," he had said.

"Do you know how to work with them?" James asked.

"Does anyone?" Teagan responded.

A deer had been brought in earlier that day. Teagan said he'd give carving a try. The committee told him to break down the deer in its entirety, from nose to tail.

"Keep the skin intact," Abe said. "We're going to need it."

Teagan hoisted the deer onto the table. He grunted and pulled at the weight. The dead look in the deer's eyes made James's stomach lurch. He didn't have any books to read, but the stories he once told haunted him now more than ever. Blood looked the same, whether dripping from a deer or waterfalling out of a person's head wound or settled in the snow after being ravaged by scavengers.

Teagan's sister Autry wanted to watch. "He's my brother and I want to help." The table held the dead deer. An open hole was in its neck where blood had seeped onto its pelt, from when the deer had been shot days ago. Autry saw the blood that had stained the deer's fur. "Is that—? I don't think I can . . ."

"She's going to pop," Charlotte said.

"I got her," Elise said. "I never liked knives." She took Autry outside to let the cold air settle the girl's stomach.

Teagan took the carving knife, still sharp from its last useful days on the ship, a dear tool to whoever had owned it previously. Teagan was ten years old. He held the knife like a broken bottle, unsure how to grip it against its sharp edges.

They had already bled the deer, soaked it in

snow for three days to let the blood drain with the water, and cleaned the pelt. Teagan held the deer on its back, its hooves in the air above the boy's head. He pressed the knife gently into the deer, near the balls, and cut, slicing up to the rib cage. His brow furrowed; beads of sweat formed from the heat and concentration.

"Why don't you cut harder?" Tic-Tac asked.

"I don't want to hit the stomach," Teagan said.

"What happens if you hit the stomach?" Tic-Tac asked.

"It can puncture, and bile and other stuff could taint the meat."

"Duh," Sarah said. She nudged Tic-Tac's shoulder.

"Oh," Tic-Tac said. "Duh."

He flipped the deer on its side and the guts spilled out.

"Oh, that's disgusting." Tic-Tac said.

Teagan raised his elbow to his face and covered

his nose. James held his breath. He waited for putrescence to fill the room but it never came.

Teagan reached his bare hand into the gaping hole and pulled out all the leftover innards and viscera that remained. The stomach pouch had mucus coating the outer walls. The bowels fell to the floor with a squelch. Teagan reached deeper and deeper into the carcass until his shoulder disappeared inside the deer, his face pressed into the midsection, his cheeks puffed out, holding his breath. Tic-Tac leaned over and hurled chunks of undigested creamy oatmeal. The splash overtook the old fallen intestines. James took a deep breath; the acidic-milky perfume filled the room.

"Can we get someone in here to clean that up?" Charlotte asked.

"We can use that stuff," Teagan said, his face no longer pressed against the deer skin, his arm removed from the deer. "The meat and intestines, I mean. We can eat that. Not the other . . . stuff."

"Okay," Abe said. "You're it."

"How'd you know how to do that?" James asked Teagan as they walked out of the room.

"The Internet," Teagan said.

"Naturally."

Someone came to mop up Tic-Tac's vomit and the ungulate's squirted mucus. That night, the Fornlanders had deer for dinner. Teagan had a new pelt to make into a blanket.

The animals that came in were hunted; more kids somehow rose to the occasion, tracking down the deer already on the island. Consistent rations came in. Autry ended up working in the greenhouse. She was close enough to her brother and was able to get filthy in the soil. Charlotte took her out one day to collect seeds that had fallen from the trees or frozen beneath the snow, under the soil, or still in the trees. Elise had wanted to go with them.

"It's not personal," Charlotte said. They all sat around the committee table. "It's just that the greenhouse is kind of my thing, my pet project."

"I get it," Elise said. "I just . . . "

"I need someone who can work with me, or on their own if I can't be there," Charlotte said.

James had watched the two leave the settlement without wandering too far. Autry wrapped herself from head to toe in puffy, purple, winter gear. She had trouble keeping up with Charlotte, taking two steps for every one Charlotte took, with a side-waddle to account for the swollen pants and jacket. Her strawberry-blonde hair was tucked into her coat. Even from the distance, James knew Charlotte tried not to laugh. Charlotte told James about their days in the forest and filling up the greenhouse.

They took two humongous pots from the kitchen, meant for stocks and soups, over three feet in diameter each.

"It's so warm in here," Autry said when they entered the greenhouse. "And so green!"

"When was the last time you saw this much green in one place?" Charlotte asked.

"Never. Not ever."

They filled different pots with dirt they took from far beneath the frozen surface.

"Why did we have to dig so deep?" Autry asked. Soil smeared across her nose. She had taken off the marshmallow jacket. Her pants squeaked when she walked and didn't waddle.

"Nutrients," Charlotte said. "The deeper we dig, the more nutrients may not have been affected by the cold. The topsoil is finished, but beneath that layer of ice there could be good soil there . . . we hope." They mixed the earth with some water. They tried to make it soft and rich. They pressed the seeds shallow into the pots.

"Now what do we do?" Autry asked.

"We wait. It doesn't hurt to hope a bit too." Beneath Autry's dirt-smothered face she had rosy cheeks and a bright smile. She may have been smiling because she liked getting dirty.

Deciding who could be a doctor was harder than finding the butcher or a glorified farmer; it was harder than any other decision they had to make.

"We could choose Geoff," James said.

Everyone stared at him coldly. No one liked Geoff. His parents didn't even like him, but that wasn't saying much when they had all ended up in an orphanage. None of their parents had liked them enough to stick around.

"Think about it," James said. "If he kills a bunch of kids, we can finally put him out of our misery."

"I like where your head's at, Hamez," Abe said. "But honestly, I say Rudy. No one ever beat him at a game of Operation."

"That's your basis?" Charlotte asked. Her hair had grown. The white color that once brushed against her shoulders now ran down to her chest. James wanted the meeting to be over so they could rush back to their room. It wasn't a secret they were together; she had nursed him back to health after he fell into the water. Only his cough remained.

Every time they were in a committee, James thought Charlotte ignored him. She deserved to be in the room more than he did. She was smarter and more well-rounded than him, even if she didn't know what the word ironic meant. She had programmed their coordinates toward Indonesia, even though they didn't make it. They ended up on an island no one knew about; even Robert had said so. James wanted to be as sure of himself as she was of herself. He was sure of her; that helped.

"I'm glad that our best bet at medicine is going to be the guy that bested the boardinghouse at Operation," Charlotte said.

"Steady hands," Abe said. James knew this was his best side, the side that showed no fear in leadership. He made the toughest decisions seem easy. It helped keep them all from cracking under the pressure of knowing that their survival depended on the decisions they made. James thought Abe cracked jokes on purpose to make it all less fatalistic, but even as Abe's best friend, he just didn't know.

Tic-Tac had told the committee the story of how Rudy pulled the glass from Claire's eye while the cruise ship was in motion. No one wanted to bring it up now for the gruesome details it involved.

"Rudy it is?" Abe asked.

"Of course it's Rudy," Charlotte said. "But I don't want anyone for one minute thinking it's because he was the best at Operation."

When Rudy helped Claire, he had given out pills like candy. The committee hoped it was because he just didn't know how else to calm her down; none of them did at the time. But Rudy had risen to the occasion and became some sort of twisted hero, and that's what the settlement needed, a group of perverse heroes, because everyone knew they weren't going to get any outstanding ones.

When they first settled the island, construction and life had gone well. The walls were built, the heat was connected, and they had enough food to last them until the greenhouse started to produce. Rudy and Buck saw to the kids who had deep gashes from sawing wood or smashed bones from missed hammer-hits; Rudy had already been the community doctor in all but name. When Rudy saw Teagan after a slip up with a freshly sharpened knife and a deer that proved too heavy, the committee made it official.

"Where's the tip?" Rudy asked Teagan.

"I brought it with," Teagan said. He pulled the tip of his index finger out of his pocket. No tears streaked down his face, and there was no indication that his fingertip had been sliced clean off except for the fistful of snow he held in his other hand with patches of red seeped through. Rudy pulled a loose thread from Teagan's shirt, burned the tip of a needle, threaded the needle, and stitched Teagan's finger back together. That night Fornland had deer for dinner and Rudy had been given a new deer-pelt blanket.

Weeks went by and James noticed a sallow look in Rudy's cheeks. Buck had it too, but James assumed it was from Buck doing some sort of work. Buck had chub to lose; Rudy didn't.

More time passed and it was harder for Rudy and

Buck to keep track of their patients—which kids needed drugs, which needed their limbs wrapped, and who needed a rest from the cold. The Fornlanders had a limited supply of drugs, after all, and those drugs should have only been given in small doses to those in desperate need. The committee had explained in strict detail the types of issues that would need prescriptions.

"Shouldn't we leave room for the 'doctor's' assessment?" Charlotte had asked.

"Not when we'll never get more of what we got," Abe said.

"Eloquent," Charlotte said.

Rudy and Buck had bonded about their arrivals in Fornland, which had been three weeks apart. They had known each other from the hospital when their parents overdosed. James had read the files of everyone in the boardinghouse before they burned the papers for warmth. He would read a page before throwing it into the fire. Bernice had been the one adult James had trusted before Robert. At least she had the courage to say goodbye to James face-to-face. She had kept impeccable notes on all the kids. Maybe she had some sort of god complex, but she had been the closest thing to a god any of them would ever see.

Rudy and Buck had been in and out of hospitals, waiting for their parents' release because they had nowhere else to go. By the time Rudy and Buck hit the Corral, they were inseparable, as if no one else there understood how they felt.

They had seen drugs and what they could do. Bernice had been good at keeping that shit away from Fornland, but Bernice wasn't on the island, hadn't been on the cruise ship, and left a long time ago to take care of her own family. Abe either didn't notice or didn't want to say anything. After all, Rudy had been his choice.

"I need you to find out," Abe said. He had taken James aside, away from the ears of the committee.

"I don't think—"

"If they're stealing drugs we need to find out now

and not when it's too late," Abe said. "Did we ever even take stock of how much there was to begin with?"

"You had left that job to Rudy."

"Fuck, I know. You don't need to remind me. If we run out, it's our ass."

"But stealing's against the rules," James said. He tried to hide the sarcasm.

Abe pressed closer to James. He lowered his voice and the anger seeped through. "You're fucking-*a* right it is. If they're stealing, everyone's going to know what happens when you break the rules."

James went to speak with Claire. After her run-in with the shard from the broken chandelier, James noticed she volunteered as much as she could at the infirmary.

"It's a form of transference," Charlotte had said. "From plight to appreciation."

"A form of what, now?" James asked.

"Transference. Rudy helped her, maybe even

saved her life. She then sees him as a savior, or something like that."

"Why do you know that?"

"Florence Nightingale. It's an entire complex."

"Really?"

"And a reality TV show," she said.

Claire kept her hair up; she said it was to keep it out of her face when helping "patients." She wore an eye patch. No one knew where she got it. In some freak accident of awesome, her eye healed with a reminiscent scar on her cornea, but she hadn't stopped wearing the patch since Rudy told her she looked badass with it on. Maybe Charlotte had a point, but it could have been another rumor in the slew of rumors that never stopped flooding the settlement.

"Have you noticed how tired Rudy is lately?" James asked Claire. The bright light in the infirmary paled her skin.

"He's been seeing a lot of patients," she said. "I think he's working too hard."

Claire had a contagious anxiousness about her. Her good eye darted to the door when she faced James, if she faced James at all. She spent most of her time moving from cabinet to beds and back again, looking lost.

"It doesn't seem strange?"

"I don't know what you're talking about," Claire said. "Nothing strange at all." She straightened the bed sheets for the third time. James almost made a sight joke, but didn't. An unsettling feeling hovered over the infirmary. Claire wouldn't talk, James knew, but if he caught her off guard . . . He left the infirmary and returned later that day. The empty room felt brighter than earlier.

"Claire?" James said. "I had one more question."

He heard the sound of dropped metal clank against the floor, a crash in the air that rattled around his head. In the corner of the room he saw Claire and Rudy bent over a grim-looking body leaning against the wall.

"I found him like this," Rudy said with

exasperation, hugging his lungs. Rudy looked at Claire, then back to James. "I swear she didn't know."

Buck was stuffed into the corner, hidden from the cold, with dropped needles around his fingers and an empty vial of morphine rolling around the floor. His eyes were half closed, filled with blank white spaces. His body was limp, chin tucked into his neck. Claire took her eye patch off and her cheeks covered with tears from both eyes. It was another problem James didn't know how to deal with. No one did.

Rudy's tiredness became clear. He had been worried about Buck.

"I tried to help him," Rudy told James. "I know more about taking drugs than stopping. Something I learned from my parents, I guess." It was the most Rudy had ever spoken to James.

"You should have come to us," James said.

"For what?" Rudy asked. "So Buck could be put on trial? Who knows what that would mean?"

"You should have come to me," James said.

"You're here now," Rudy said.

"I . . . it's too late, now. Do you know how much he took?"

"Over the past couple weeks it got worse. I had kept most of the stash in my room trying to hide it."

"Did it work?" James asked.

"I had to leave some here in case Abe came in."

"What if Buck had taken it all?"

A small rattle rose from the corner. Claire had stood up and pushed an empty vial around the floor. She blushed.

"Keep her out of this," Rudy said.

"You swear she didn't know?" James asked. He tried to give some clue to Rudy that would tell him to agree, a subtle nod.

"I swear," Rudy said.

"That's not true," Claire said. "I helped move some of the vials so Buck wouldn't find them."

"Claire, stop," Rudy said. Her eye patch stayed dark against her flushed cheeks.

"I cleaned Buck up afterwards. It was my idea."

Rudy looked at James. His eyes pleaded and James understood the fear in Rudy's eyes; Rudy cared for her. He couldn't protect Buck anymore but it was clear, he wanted to protect Claire.

"That isn't true," Rudy said.

"What isn't true?" James asked. Claire and Rudy remained quiet for a moment. James listened to their quick breaths. Claire pulsed with anxiety. Rudy's chest inhaled with concentration. The room was hot and sticky. Buck sat in the corner but hovered over all of them with the presence of his actual weight on their shoulders.

"Any of it," Rudy said.

"Any of what?" James asked.

"All of—"

"You should try to keep the rumors under control," James interrupted.

"Right," Rudy said.

James left the infirmary and walked across the snow to Abe's room. He opened the door without knocking and poked his head in.

"You're bringing in the cold," Elise said.

James stepped inside and closed the door.

"Sorry," he said.

"What's going on?" Elise asked.

"Where's Abe?"

"Out doing something heroic, I'm sure." Elise rolled her eyes. The sarcasm was rich rolling off her tongue. "Checking on the progress of the greenhouse, I think."

"I can talk to him later." James went to leave but Elise moved across the room and placed her hand on James's. His fingers gripped the doorknob; her hand grazed his glove. Her skin was wrinkled from moisture. James hadn't taken off any of his winter clothes. Elise's breath smelled of mint, an aroma that reminded James of spring.

"Stay," she said. "Just a minute longer." She turned away from James and stepped back. "I just wanted to . . . I was wondering—"

James had never seen her anxious or bashful, or whatever emotion she portrayed at that moment. "Do you miss San Diego?" she asked.

"It's tough," James said. "Sometimes I miss it all and other times I can't think of anything I miss."

"I just feel like it's harder to remember anything about it except for—"

She moved closer to James again. Her minty breath returned. The closer she came, the more uncomfortable James felt. This wasn't the Elise he knew.

"It just feels like something is missing, or I'm missing something . . . "

"I think we all feel that way." James took a small step away from Elise. "I can talk to Abe later. I think you need some time to—"

"You know Abe best," she said.

"I don't think anyone knows Abe," he said. "Not really, at least not any more than you do."

"I doubt that. He's different than he used to be."

James felt it too. Ever since they had boarded the ship. The more Elise spoke the more James wanted to agree, but in some larger way he thought he needed to defend his friend.

"How so?" James asked. "I mean, he's been under a lot of pressure lately. I think he's trying—"

"To be a god," she said. Her eyes glowed fierce. "Infallible."

"That's harsh," James said.

"I know you were supposed to look into Rudy and Buck, not that Abe told me. He hasn't said much to me lately. Notice anything missing?" She looked around the room, but he couldn't see what she wanted him to see. He shrugged. "Think about what you tell him; he isn't himself."

"I need to tell him what I found," James said.

"Does he deserve to know?" Elise asked.

Abe opened the door. The force pushed James away from the entrance. The cushion from his jacket protected his shoulder.

"The greenhouse is growing," Abe said with cheeriness. "We could have real crops by—" he spotted James near the corner of the room and closed the door behind him. Abe held a bouquet of basil and mint in his hand.

"Hamez, I didn't know you were here." Abe handed Elise the bouquet but said nothing. His focus stayed on James. "Could we have a minute, Elise?"

"I can't even stay in our room?"

"We need a minute . . . "

The old bickering relationship had gone away. Abe acted like Elise was a subordinate. He acted the same way with everyone else too, James realized. Elise put on her coat and walked out. She rubbed her hand on the doorframe as she walked away. James remembered Abe and Elise's initials in San Diego, the same initials that decorated the cruise ship. Abe hadn't carved a single letter on the island. That's what Elise must have meant.

" . . . With Rudy and Buck?" Abe asked.

"What?" James asked.

"Doesn't matter. What did you find out?"

"It's hard to say," James said. What if more than Elise and Abe's initials was missing? Abe had changed, James knew, but this was a moment Abe could prove he had changed for the better and Elise's subtle disdain would disappear. In the wake of Robert's mysterious death, James didn't have much reason not to trust Abe. Adults made stupid choices; everyone did. It cost all these kids everything more than once.

James looked Abe in his cold, dark eyes and told him everything. James believed he protected everyone by telling the truth. The story unfolded and James realized he hadn't said it all. He left out Claire from the story—she was safe, but safe from what?

BECAUSE WALLS CAN'T TALK

JAMES

JAMES LAY IN BED, AND THE GEOTHERMAL SYSTEM CONTINUED to heat the homes of the new settlement. The sheets were taken from the cruise ship, as was so much else that helped them build and decorate their new life as the cruise ship had smoldered on the opposite side of the island.

"Do you think Tic-Tac and Sarah are all right?" Charlotte asked.

She stood behind a screen to change. It didn't matter how confident Charlotte was, James thought, a lack of self-esteem and body issues were second nature.

"Why?" James asked. "I haven't noticed anything."

"Tic-Tac seems distracted lately," she said. "Don't you think?" Her coat hung over the screen. James searched for a shadow in the dim light of dusk but found none.

"I thought it had to do with Claire," James said.

"I agree."

"Yeah but . . . wait. I'm not sure what we're talking about."

Charlotte's pants joined her coat over the screen. During the committee meeting earlier that day, James had tried not to look at Tic-Tac when they'd discussed problems with Rudy. James always liked Tic-Tac but could only see two things: Tic-Tac as a hero, flowing cape and all, diving into the water to save him, and Tic-Tac filled with constant fear of what happened to Claire, even though she was fine now. When Tic-Tac told James what happened, he had hesitated. "I closed my eyes. I couldn't look. I couldn't watch that. I nearly fainted or shat myself or something. I just—don't tell anyone." James understood how certain nightmares could manifest in the daylight. No matter how hard James tried, he still saw Marcus's hand outstretched for help beneath a pile of rabid scavs tearing him apart. James wanted to look at Tic-Tac like the hero James knew him to be, not shamefaced about what he couldn't do.

"Sarah told me he's been distant," Charlotte said.

"He's been busy."

"I think he has a thing for Claire. It started around the time she volunteered at the infirmary. Sarah didn't realize it, but I put the clues together." Her clothes started to pile up over the screen. James imagined how much she had left on.

He knew the real reason Tic-Tac was distant, for the same reason as James. Sometimes he felt like an imposter, unable to live up to the potential others saw in him that he couldn't see in himself. Tic-Tac was one of the bravest kids James had ever met, yet shadows of doubt washed over even him. Charlotte was the most confident girl James knew, self-aware and proud, but even she hid behind a screen when changing.

"I don't think that's it," James said.

"What do you think it is?" Charlotte asked. She stepped from behind the screen. She wore black-frilled lace. The white strands of her hair popped like snow against the smooth outline of her outfit. James had never seen lace in person. As his days in Fornland turned into years and the years turned into snow, the need for lace dissolved.

Charlotte wore nothing but black lace and a sharp smile. The candles flickered. Fornland had been making them from deer tallow and sinew, keeping whatever they had taken from the ship for emergencies.

"Where did that come from?" James asked.

"I found it on the ship," Charlotte said. "I took it in case I got hot."

"Good thinking," James said.

"I have good ideas, sometimes," she said.

"We can all use a few of those."

In the warmth of the room James could almost forget about the world's eagerness to swallow them whole. He imagined paradise and thought of snow-boarding trips that he never took. Hiking in the Alps and trekking the Himalayas. If he concentrated hard enough, the stories would spin and weave in his. But he was tired of stories. He was just tired.

Charlotte's cheeks glistened with sweat. Sweat became coveted in the eternal winter, because sweat meant warmth and warmth meant life. She swayed from side to side and the lace swished.

"You know you're beautiful, right?" James said. Charlotte blushed with the embarrassment of vulnerability.

"It's the lace," she said. "It could make an ape pretty."

"If I saw an orangutan in a frilly nighty I'd probably agree. Then wonder where the nighty came from. Then wonder where the orangutan came from." He would never understand the line she drew between her confidence and insecurities. James called Charlotte beautiful, in the same way he called the sun beautiful—he never could look at the sun for too long before turning away. James started to think of the gray clouds more like cobwebs that covered the sky because the sun wasn't using the space anymore. The sky was out of date and abandoned.

When the Northern Lights started flashing across the night sky, he had to amend his idea, but even those had disappeared. His cough tore through the room. Charlotte stood against the screen with a small smile James couldn't place, somewhere between uncertainty and cunning. They often bordered each other. Something was off about the moment. The lace too big, her frame too small, the way she posed—calculated. She looked like a girl playing dress-up, rather than a woman. James felt he spent too much time pretending to be an adult, but if he pretended long enough, he could at least feel like one, like the way he'd attempted to mask the snowy expanse as a needed vacation. How long could he pretend before the lies took their toll?

Charlotte sashayed to the bed. She pressed her

hands to the sheets, pressed her knees to the mattress. Her hair draped her face, the smile stayed, slick and cool. She pressed her lips to James's. Her mouth was warm. Her tongue was soft. He forgot about Tic-Tac and about Marcus. He forgot about Claire and Sarah and Fornland. There was Charlotte. Lace tickled his neck. Her lips pressed against his lips. Her hand rested on his chest, her warm body against his warm body. The room created a heat wave that washed over them, where they cooled each other with kisses. For a moment he forgot about everything else.

James couldn't sleep and watched the empty spaces on the ceiling blend into the night's dark. Earlier the settlement had asked for another story, one the kids had heard countless times before. It was a story the kids drew strength from. It was the first story James ever told. They all sat in the dining room after the dishes were washed and the tables were cleaned. Tic-Tac and Sarah snuggled up together. Some kids hid for momentary seclusion. Others focused on James, gathering every word.

"The children were collected like rocks, hardened and resilient from the elements," James said. "Not from thrashing wind or pounding waves or bolts of lightning."

Some kids added sound effects to the story. They *crashed* and *wooshed* with the elements to give everyone a deeper visual.

"We were shaped by the elements of humanity."

The room erupted in boos.

"People destroyed one another and the world by malice or by accident. We came from a world where the rocks and the children could survive for another decade as the world tore itself apart from the inside out.

"The intestines of the earth were strewn about by lava and earthquakes, drowned by tidal waves, torn open by hurricanes and tornadoes. The elements hardened the rocks and placed us at Samuel S. Fornland Boardinghouse, where those rocks polished into children. The rocks grew in their resilience but stayed tender in their hearts toward one another, in a world ravaged by its own claws."

The room filled with uproarious applause at the mention of them as survivors, not victims.

"The first child was born of a boulder, carved out of the mountainside that had fallen into the Pacific. Waves rolled over her, salt crusted her, wind personalized her, and she washed onto San Diego's shores like so many discarded tires, the sun beating down on her skin. Her hair looked like a mat; she reeked of feral water. Her skin swam with olive pit colors. She carved out a cave in Fornland. Every day she walked the beaches, picking up rocks along the shore, and throwing them into the water. Some sank, overtaken by starfish and crustaceans. Other rocks were pushed back on shore as children. Time passed and Fornland was filled with these children from the sea."

"That's us!" Teagan shouted.

"Sit down," Shia said.

"Of course it's us," Geoff grumbled.

"But, as with time and children, all things change and all life grows."

A small groan came from the crowd. James knew they all hated this part the most. James wondered if he changed the story, if he stopped speaking of passing time, could he change what happened? He couldn't help but wonder how many of the others thought the same thing.

"These children grew and left Fornland ready to settle in the world that had broken them into shards to begin with; this time they were harder, fiercer, and ready for the wear and tear of society.

"Except for the boulder. She was alone again and found herself along the sea, throwing rocks into the water, her hair back to woven straw, her body as young and sharp as ever. More rocks were shaped, more rocks were children, more children came to Fornland, more children grew and entered the world.

"The boulder was tired and lonely, was tired of being lonely, because the friends and family she had made all left her for a world she couldn't understand. She tried to settle herself back onto the cliff where she had first fallen but the rocks refused her. She tried to fit into the rush of the city, but they called her slow and young and stupid, a punk kid, a know-it-all—she hid in Fornland until a building grew around her. Now and again, a lost child stumbled through the doors in search of shelter and she would call to them, soothe them until they were cared for, until they were ready to move on."

"That's where we come from," Claire said. Her voice was timid but her face held pride.

"Damn right," Abe said.

"That is why we are here," James said. "Because the walls themselves cared for us. A home for the abandoned, because we cried too much, didn't use our words, because we never grew up enough and were thrown out like a handful of rocks. Those walls eventually led us here, to this wonderland, taking shape beneath the snow. You may not love it—but you're home."

The room stayed quiet until Abe stood up and said, "I love it here." Shia's smaller voice followed, "I love it here." More voices littered the room, each one imitating Abe's empowering call. James watched the kids with admiration. They looked at one another believing they were born and bred to live. They stood up empowered by the story, by the lies, and by Abe. *They truly love it here*, James thought. *If only I felt the same.*

Now he lay in bed stroking Charlotte's arm, anticipating the moment she sprung up from a nightmare. He would help calm her down, reassure her, kiss her forehead, and stop feeling useless.

TREES DON'T PAY ATTENTION

TIC-TAC

THE TREE LINE LOOKED DIFFERENT AT DUSK. THE CANOPY darkened when the gray sky churned into black, like the canopy rose upwards into the atmosphere and tried to kiss the starlight. Tic-Tac stood yards away from the fern forest. The sounds of the settlement were far enough to be muddled but continued to fill nightfall. He was stuffed inside his heavy coat that felt heavier since they left San Diego, knowing it was a weight he was forced to continually carry.

"It's a bit cold out," Sarah said.

Tic-Tac had heard her footsteps and ignored them. He knew they were hers from her simple but focused stride.

"Dinner will be ready soon."

He didn't move, keeping his eyes on the tree line to watch the night wash over the island. The colors in the sky matured from San Diego when blues, oranges, reds, and yellows littered the open space from horizon to horizon. Three shades existed in the sky now: day gray, night blue, and fading starry-yellow. The Northern Lights left months ago as if they had frozen with the rest of the world. The nature of cold confounded Tic-Tac. How could it overrun something as vast as the world and endure? A living thing among living things that spread, took away life, and tested the lives of anyone that had the misfortune of surviving . . .

"I think we're having some sort of tomato thing," Sarah said. "It smelled delicious. I mean, as delicious as it could be, you know . . . you know your way around the kitchen. Those kids learned a lot from you."

Howls crept into the night sky. The dogs had become more aggressive in their vocals. They hadn't made their way into the settlement, but in the heart of the night, the Fornlanders heard the cries and wondered if the dogs came closer. When the dogs cried, it echoed the sounds that used to fill the Corral when a new kid had found his new bed in a new place vastly different from what his home had been.

"Sometimes I wonder if the man on the moon is a bunch of bullshit," Tic-Tac said.

"That's what the dogs are calling to," Sarah said. "That's the story James told, remember? The dogs cry out because the man used to give them food. Then he died of old age, but they cast him into the sky so he could always look down on them. Every night they call out to him because they miss him. He smiles down on them because he's watching."

"I don't think I can believe that anymore," Tic-Tac said.

"Since when?" Sarah rubbed her hands over her arms. Tic-Tac wanted to wrap his arms around her and hold her close. He wished he could keep her warm with his hands on hers. He stared at the trees instead, waiting for the moon. "You loved those stories."

"I did," Tic-Tac said. "But you ever think they're just stories? They aren't filled with people or lives or far-off places or magic. They're all just fantasy."

Sarah leaned her shoulder into Tic-Tac. He could feel her hot breath on his neck. She gently pressed her slightly chapped lips to his skin.

"Why is that bad?" she whispered into his ear. The dark crawled slowly down from the sky and covered the gray. "It doesn't have to be real to be liked."

"What does it teach us?" His voice rang out in the open space between them and the forest where the howls rose.

Sarah pulled away. She shoved her hands into her pockets. "You want to learn something? Follow Teagan around and cut up a deer."

"I just don't think—"

"No, you're not. What's going on with you? I haven't gone anywhere but you keep looking past me like you'll find whatever it is that's bugging you somewhere behind me, or in the forest, or . . . or . . . in me. Is that it? Is it me?"

A gust of wind brushed over the snow. Flakes lifted and landed in the strands of Sarah's hair that weren't hidden beneath her beanie. Some flakes landed on Tic-Tac's cheek. He wiped them away and reached for her. He wanted to brush away the snow with her agitation. He wanted to brush away the cold with her sadness. He wanted to travel back in time to before this wretched existence. First it was the snow, then the scavs, then the ice, the ship, the dome. He couldn't escape the blood, no matter how hard he tried; it just always showed up. Instead of breaking him down, he felt hardened. A brick wall was constructed around his heart, growing thicker, even when he couldn't escape the screams of their curdled pasts. He grabbed Sarah's hand.

"It isn't you in any way," he said.

"I'm here. Is it just the stories? It's hard to lose something you believe in."

"I never believed the stories." He gripped her hand tighter. "I believed the endings. Pinocchio became a real boy. The princess kissed the prince. Superman saved the day. We could be whatever we wanted to be."

"That isn't wrong."

"It's always been wrong."

Sarah wrapped her arms around Tic-Tac. Sometimes in the heat of their hugs, Tic-Tac felt the snow melt a little beneath them. Steam rose from their bodies in blissful connection. For this brief second the walls around him shrank a little.

"It's truer now more than ever." She stood on her toes to reach his face. Her hot breath tickled his ear. The world was dark. The tree line blended into the sky. Sarah grabbed his hand.

He hoped she was right, but the longer they stood in the cold, the walls rebuilt inside of him.

"I just liked the stories," he said.

"Let's go to dinner," she said and started to lead him back to the settlement where the cries of boisterous kids overtook the howls from the forest.

FRESH FRAGRANCE
NEARING

ELISE

THE FORNLANDERS COULDN'T DENY THE RANCID SCENT THAT came from most of the older kids. Everyone wanted to be in a warm, dry place, but with the heat came sweat, and with sweat came body odor. Nancy Daron was twelve years old and for a while, cornered the settlement's black market making deodorant. The problem became her use of resources taken from the ship. Elise had heard Nancy even stole deodorant from the reserves. People started to trade goods: socks, underwear, food, soap, et cetera.

Elise met Nancy three years ago—before all the snow fell. Elise was thirteen; Nancy was nine and brand new to Fornland. Everyone called her Daron,

anyone that noticed her at least. She was an I.C.—
Invisible Child—one of many used to blending into
big crowds, hiding in plain sight, usually because
of a drunk or perverted relative. It helped Daron
with her father while her mother turned away and
ignored it all. An I.C. would become so ingrained
in their invisibility they couldn't stop even if they
wanted to.

"You're Daron?" Elise had asked.

"Who are you?" Daron responded.

"I'm Elise." Elise heard Daron had struggled with
school and getting settled, the usual issues of the
abandoned and broken. "I want to show you something."

Elise took Daron to the unit where James was
reading. That was where Elise had first met Abe,
when she heard James read a story and change
Fornland into someplace exotic. It was a place
Daron could listen without being seen.

"'Once upon a time there was a piece of wood,'"

James had said. A group of kids surrounded James while he read, including Tic-Tac and Abe.

"You ever hear of Pinocchio?" Elise asked. Daron shook her head. "I think you'll like him."

Daron sat down and blended into the small group. Elise saw her big brown eyes and short ponytail. She saw the children, invisible or not, because one thing was true for everyone in Fornland, especially the new: they were all lonely.

In the new settlement the Fornlanders made on the island, the committee had an emergency meeting to crack down on the raiding of supplies.

"There's no excuse," Abe said. "It's out of control. We shouldn't have to put locks on the doors. We shouldn't have this mistrust of one another. It's done. No more of this sh—stuff."

"Except," Charlotte said, "we kind of need it." No one nodded along but everyone agreed. "This place reeks. I never feel clean. If it isn't our bodies it's our clothes. If not this stuff, we need something."

"I can talk to her," Elise said.

"It's too late for talking." Abe said. "She stole from the reserves!"

"That's a rumor," Elise said. "We don't know if that actually happened."

"When rumors gain momentum . . . " James said.

"We know," the committee said in unison, Elise's forceful voice at the forefront.

"I just mean—" James said.

"Couldn't we talk to her . . . ?" Elise asked.

"I'm with Elise," Charlotte said.

"Fine," Abe said. "She has one day or we're talking about punishment." Elise was left alone in the warm stink of the committee room.

That night Elise confronted Daron in her combined room that she shared with two other girls. Elise knew all of them. They sat on Daron's floor. The room smelled pleasantly of herbs, not like the stale terror of most rooms.

"Cold?" Elise asked. No one was cold anymore

in the settlement but the greeting had stayed from when the snow first fell. "It smells nice in here."

"One of the few places that isn't ripe with shit," Daron said.

"You know I don't like when you talk that way," Elise said.

"The other kids—"

"That makes it better?"

"Okay. I'm sorry."

"You need to stop," Elise said.

"I said I was sorry."

"With the deodorant. You need to stop. If you don't, the next conversation we have will be very different."

"Is that a threat?" Daron asked.

"I'm trying to help," Elise said. "People need this but you have to find another way. I heard ash and animal fat work."

"What?"

The next day Daron stopped passing deodorant

around. The rumors spread fast, as rumors always did.

"She must've been threatened," a tall, graceful girl said.

"I think they figured out who she was," a squat, round-faced boy said.

"I heart that stuff causes lumps," Shia said. A small group of boys nodded. Elise noticed a full day of random people scratching at their armpits.

The stink almost re-emerged but Daron started to make soap from tallow and ash. It kept people clean and didn't use any of Fornland's resources.

"This is good," Abe said. For the first time since the settlement was built, the scent of a room didn't twist people's stomachs. There were some smells people became used to, but somehow the Fornlanders couldn't get used to their own stink.

TRYING PATIENCE

CHARLOTTE

THE VILLAGE SURROUNDED THE ICEDOME IN A QUIET STUPOR. It was the first trial the settlement had ever staged. Buck and Rudy stood in the center of the dome. Buck looked slack jawed and exhausted. Rudy held a similar tiredness displayed in the deep shadows under his eyes. Charlotte watched with a mixture of fascination and horror in anticipation of an inescapable destruction soon to come.

Abe stood at the ledge of the dome and looked into the pit. James stood behind Abe and occasionally whispered in Abe's ear. Elise stood near Charlotte. The longer the trial went on, the closer Elise inched to Charlotte.

"I told him to keep it to himself," Elise muttered under her breath.

"The whole thing?" Charlotte asked. She hadn't known if Elise spoke to her or not. Elise nodded.

The cold air rose from the ground and spread across the sky. Rudy looked stoic next to Buck and resembled a child. Buck was always big for his age, which made people think he was mature, but size wasn't everything.

"I doubt this will turn out well," Elise said.

Charlotte turned to the proceedings. Buck stared at the ground. Abe had stated the grievances against Buck. "Stolen goods, illicit usage, and the worst offense," Abe had said, "pure selfishness without regard for the settlement."

Rudy had tried to plead for Buck—Buck's addiction.

"Most of us have seen what addiction can do," Rudy said. "It caused poor decisions. Buck and I know that firsthand. You," Rudy looked at Abe, "should understand."

Charlotte felt a rush of pity wash over her. Abe would not appreciate being compared to those two, put on trial for breaking the rules and for disobeying.

"Addiction takes over—"

"That's enough," Abe said.

Elise wrapped her arm through Charlotte's and gripped tight.

"Can Buck speak for himself?" Abe asked.

Buck shrugged and never looked up from the ground. *If he values his life, he needs to speak up*, Charlotte thought. The intensity emanating from the trial was palpable to everyone watching. However, Charlotte felt her and Elise were the only two that fully understood the possibility of the outcome. Charlotte tried to be pragmatic, but sometimes her mind jumped to the worst possible conclusion. That feeling had become stronger since they landed on the island.

"If he has nothing to say," Abe said, "then we will talk about the verdict."

Abe called the committee together beside the dome.

"He's guilty and has no argument," Abe said.

"We can be lenient," Elise said.

"He's stolen morphine," Abe said. "That sh— stuff is important and we only had a limited supply to begin with."

"I agree with Elise," Charlotte said. The crowd grumbled and grew restless. She looked back at Rudy and Buck. Rudy patted his friend's back and said something Charlotte couldn't hear.

"Mercy isn't weakness," Elise said.

"He needs help, I think," Tic-Tac said.

"Maybe a small punishment," Shia said before recoiling behind Abe.

Abe turned to the dome and looked at Buck.

"It's decided," Abe said. "Buck, for stealing morphine from the infirmary this committee has decided a light punishment." A sigh of relief fell over the settlement.

"That's not fair," Geoff screamed. "He broke—"

Abe held up his hand and Geoff quieted down.

"But for putting yourself before the settlement, I sentence you to death."

Elise gasped. The sound shattered the encircling shock. James shook his head. Catcalls and cheers, jeers and boos spread around the kids. Abe spoke above the noise.

"And for your part in aiding Buck, Rudy, you are sentenced to five lashes."

"Wait a minute," James said. "You can't."

"Can't what?" Abe asked.

James backed down. Charlotte had not seen him so dejected since the day Marcus died. *Sometimes it isn't in us to fight*, Charlotte thought.

Three guards entered the dome to lead Buck away. When a fourth guard arrived with the whip, Buck sprung to life. Buck threw one guard to the ground and kicked another.

"Stop it!" Rudy shouted. No one listened. More guards swarmed the dome. Two pulled Rudy away as he kicked and screamed, his usual calm demeanor all but forgotten. The remaining guards rushed Buck and pulled him to the ground. They beat him with clubs. Buck tried to push himself up but fell back to the ground. The crowd cheered, their earlier concern giving way to amusement. Two guards held Rudy against the wall. Buck lay motionless and bleeding on the icy ground.

"We'll clean him up and continue," a stout guard said.

"No," Abe said. "Do it now."

The crowd cheered. Each sound defied disgust. Elise had stopped watching. James watched with his chin held high; Charlotte knew it was his shamed look, pretending to be better than what he saw. He spent too much time waiting to play the hero, but he never stood up when it was needed most.

The guards pulled off Rudy's coat, sweater, and shirt. His skin was much paler than his face. One guard yielded the whip. Abe had asked Charlotte to make one.

"Why would we need a whip?" she had asked.

"Can you make one or not?" Abe responded.

"No," she lied. Shia had known and offered instead. He took excess rope they had removed from the ship. Shia measured lengths of around five feet long, looping each measure back and measuring again. He made an image of a star out of the rope and folded the points over to touch one another. He then folded the rope over once more and made a three-inch knot. He continued to loop the rope until making another knot around the handle approximately six inches from the base. Charlotte had reluctantly witnessed the process, fascinated by Shia's resolve and focus. He finished and flicked a true, dangerous whip.

Now, in the dome, Rudy was on his knees with his face pressed to the wall. Two guards held his arms out in a "T," pressing his elbows to the wall. They leaned away from Rudy's body to escape the coming blows.

The guard pulled the whip back and swung it side-armed. The sickening snap of the whip mixed with a blood-curdling crack of Rudy's skin. He bit into his lip to hide his screams. On the second lash Charlotte saw blood drip from Rudy's mouth, self-inflicted.

On the fifth lash the guards let Rudy fall to the ground, back torn open in striations. The extra guards dragged Buck out of the dome, leaving a smeared trail of his own blood, which no one wanted to follow.

COLD METALLIC SKIN

ELISE

ELISE SAT AT THE EDGE OF HER BED, A KNIFE IN HER HANDS.
All eating utensils had been restricted to the kitchen areas. Abe had created the rule shortly after the settlement had built the kitchen, since resources were limited. The settlement could cut trees for shelter and use the metal from the ship to help weld pipes. Robert had taught the settlement how to heat the metal in the fire and hammer the edges together, like blacksmiths in the Middle Ages. The settlement used the pipes to transfer heat from the hot springs to each home. They dug drop toilets with shovels and used wood, mud, and sticks to make shelter. They made a community. But they couldn't replace

lost goods because they couldn't forge metal. They couldn't quarry for rocks. Trees wouldn't replenish. They couldn't walk to the store and buy new spoons when someone broke, bent, or misplaced one. The arbitrary utensils of their pasts in San Diego became coveted. Anything used for eating couldn't leave the kitchen at all; the implements were pulled out before meals and locked up afterward. People could have eaten with their hands, but Elise wanted to maintain a modicum of civility in this uncivilized place. Elise tried to hold onto the sense of decency they had all known when younger.

The night before, James and Elise had been in the kitchen helping Daron clean up after making soap. The process was similar to making candles, which had given Elise the idea to consolidate the two. Four kids had been set to the task. With the daylight winding down, the kids left and James helped Elise with the rest of the pots.

"They still aren't up," Elise said. She put the pot on a high shelf across the room to make sure no one would confuse the candle and soap pots with the cooking pots.

"The new baths?" James asked. "They should be up soon."

"The initials," Elise said. "I know he's busy but . . ."

Abe had first carved their initials into wet cement outside of Fornland when they started dating. When the snow covered the cement, he carved their initials in the snow every day.

"He has been doing a lot," James said. "I'm sure he's thinking about it, just hasn't had a chance."

"You keep saying that. You can't make excuses for him all the time."

"I don't make excuses for him," James said. "Besides, it's hard to get a knife around here." James smiled an uneasy smile.

A quiet joke between old friends, Elise thought. Abe did what he wanted now. It was obvious to her Abe didn't want her anymore, or he would have carved their initials like he said he would. But his place, and this life, made people forget.

"It's not that hard," Elise whispered.

"You can't leave with that," James said.

"I think you overestimate him," Elise said. "He's changed since San Diego."

"I know," James said. "I'm sure he'll change back."

"That's not how it works," Elise said. "Look what he did to Buck and Rudy. He was so close to throwing Daron in the jail block. And Lily . . . " her voice trailed off as she looked to the door.

Shia ran into the kitchen, nodded at Elise, and said, "James? Abe needs to talk to you about the new baths." He stood by the door and waited.

James held up a hand to Shia but otherwise didn't acknowledge him. "It's not easy for anyone," James said. Shia stayed quiet and out of sight. "These are the rules. We all agreed—"

"I didn't agree!" Elise screamed. She slid the knife inside her pocket hiding inside her parka. "Not to this and not to the snow." Elise threw down the last pan. James didn't move. She stormed out of the kitchen and back to her room where she found the knife in her jacket.

Now the knife was hers. Elise ran her finger along its serrated edge. The blade tore at her skin; she didn't react. The heat in her room was comfy. The warm blood dripped to the floor. She had cheered when the snow started to fall. She looked back at those moments with nostalgia for when each fallen snowflake was a lifetime away—each snowflake a different, infinite life.

She rubbed the flat edge of the knife to feel the cold metal on her wrist. She turned the blade toward her skin and felt the warm trickle of plasma replace her frozen hand. It dripped down to her fingers, hot and wet, different from the cold that hadn't lifted. She never meant to cut deep. She just wanted to feel something warm around her, again, in some way.

She sat at the edge of her bed in a cozy room on a frozen island. She rubbed the flat surface of the stolen knife against her skin. She thought of herself at Fornland, her first weeks, her first words to Abe, the first second she separated her skin with a knife. Abe ignored life and James stared at a stupid book as if it would bring a dead kid back to life. Nothing came back and no one came back. Why would they want to?

The world was dying. Elise wouldn't wait around. She couldn't imagine another life after this one, after they had escaped so much already. How much more could be left for them? Her reflection in the steel knife reminded her of her mother, except this time Elise wasn't hopeful; she felt deceived.

For a brief second she relished the cold steel. She dropped the knife. Hot blood rushed out of her—downstream. It leaked over her fingertips, falling to the floor. She dreamed of conversations she never had with kids she had never met. The room started to spin. The air turned stony against her exposed skin.

"There's just too much blankness." She tried to

justify the world to herself. "Even darkness would help." She closed her eyes to escape the nausea. Her body relaxed, no longer rigid against the mattress and sheets. The spicy scent of mint drifted around the room. Images of her and Abe's initials flashed in the darkness.

The little trickle of blood shifted into a flood. She had been tired for years. She had fought for longer than she needed to. What would the frozen world look like tomorrow? She didn't care. She wouldn't see it. She lay her head on the pillow and felt its plushness. A wave of exhaustion rushed over her. She accepted it and fell asleep.

SILENT IMPERFECTIONS

JAMES

WHEN JAMES ENTERED THE ROOM, ABE'S FACE WAS pressed against Elise's body, her coat full around her shoulders. Her head tilted back, her eyes stared at the ceiling as if she had left a question there she wanted answered. Abe's face rested against her chest, which housed an inaudible noise, hiding his pain, his tears, his everything. From where James stood, the bed blocked her wrists. Her chest brushed wet blood against Abe's body, staining his clothes with the last memories of her that he would ever have.

How could the settlement not hear the

thunderous silence that sounded so loud to James? The scream was in his head. Abe's cries were real.

The last time he heard Abe cry was the first time he heard Abe cry; it was years ago. Adoption was painful in Fornland between the ages of six and ten. They were young enough to be cute and didn't know enough about attitude to spit at would-be-parents. Once a month some kids paraded through the halls like peacocks, dressed to the nines. They waited at the door with their colorful plumage stuck out in pomp without circumstance.

James and Abe thought they knew better: the kids weren't peacocks in the field; they were all puppies in the pound in search of the one family that would take pity on an animal bound for euthanasia. James had a theory that more kids weren't adopted because no matter how much people disliked or ignored orphans, an orphan would never be euthanized. It was a saving grace and damnation all at the same time.

Abe, like James, never thought he'd be picked up

by some stray couple. They didn't bother strutting their feathers but they held onto some faint glimmer of hope. Why else would they have stuck around on P-D—Pick-up Day? Most six-cells headed out to the movies or the beach or a park or sulked in their rooms until the circus went away and the kids changed into clothes a little more appropriate for a young orphan. Abe and James held out in the common rooms and read, played Connect Four, or sometimes played Operation in a silent agreement to see if the noise would bring attention their way. It didn't.

Abe was almost picked up on a day when nothing out of the ordinary happened. They sat in the common room in their normal clothes. Abe wore a simple black shirt and jeans, a style he tried to emulate from his father—another secret James knew but never brought up. James wore a plaid button-down and khakis because he liked how they breathed. They were sitting on the floor next to the "library," which was no more than a collection of thirty books untouched by most of the boardinghouse.

"What are you reading?" the man asked Abe.

Abe didn't flinch and looked up. He held up the cover for the man to see. *Matilda.*

"One of my favorites," the man said. "How do you like it?" Abe shrugged. "Wish you had magic powers?"

"Who doesn't?" Abe said.

"What would you do if you could move things with your mind?"

"I'd take some chocolate," Abe said.

"Chocolate?"

Abe pulled half a Snickers from his pocket. James had given it to him earlier that morning. Abe put it on the book and made it look like he hadn't used his hands.

"See?" Abe said. "Chocolate."

"One hell of a magic trick," the man said.

The trick didn't impress James. The trick didn't impress the man either, but he feigned fascination.

James wasn't the type to get involved with Loos—people that came in and *looked* at the kids like zoo animals. James didn't like to go to the zoo at all; he knew how the animals felt. He wanted to be happy for Abe, who wasn't one to talk to Loos either, but he didn't feel happy. He wanted the man to walk away and leave them alone with their books and their goddamn boardinghouse.

"Want to try again for a full one?" the man asked.

"I'm not hungry," Abe said. The man laughed.

Later that day they brought Abe into the office—the man, another man, and Bernice. James wasn't allowed inside. He spent the afternoon on the same floor reading over *Matilda* for the third time in some desperate attempt to take Abe's place, where if he read the words over and over the man would come back upstairs and take James too, or instead.

Instead! It hit James like a train. He never thought about P-D, but he would have rather have been in the room with two people he didn't know than with his best friend pressing the metal tweezers against the rim of operation, no longer to get people's attention but to see how long the game could buzz before it broke.

The sun was almost down before Abe walked by. He passed through the hallway and went straight to his bed. He crumpled like a candy wrapper, his knees to his chest. James sat on Abe's bed. The Corral was empty. Kids didn't like other people sitting on their bed uninvited, when their beds were their one piece of personal space. Most of the time James didn't care but this time he cared for a different reason. The bed bounced and the springs twanged in the quiet. Abe sniffed.

"They didn't want me," Abe said.

"You were in the room," James said. "He liked the candy trick."

Abe didn't wipe at the tears that ran into the sheets. His eyes were red. The sun was red as it burnt itself into darkness.

"Bernice told them how long it would take," Abe said.

"How long what would take?"

"They liked me well enough to take home but not to wait for."

"It would have been hard—"

"Now you don't have to worry about it." Abe blinked the tears away, running down his cheeks and turning the light sheets murky. Night had blanketed San Diego but the streetlights hadn't come on yet.

"I was worried that I'd be here alone." Rain started to tap against the window. There hadn't been a report on rain. "Again."

Everyone knew if you weren't picked up by ten years old, you wouldn't be. James had told Abe that he didn't care to get picked up. It was true at the time. It was true now because Abe was still around. It wasn't true during the three hours he thought Abe would leave.

"Guess you don't have to worry," Abe said.

"At least—"

"Don't," Abe said. "I don't need an at least. Just . . . a minute."

James stood up. Abe's cries ran in sniffles and body shakes. The bed squeaked. The rain fell.

The next morning Abe was back to smiles. James almost asked, almost consoled. Instead they sat on the floor with Operation between them. Abe pressed the metal tweezers to the side of the heart. The game buzzed. It buzzed, and buzzed, until James and Abe couldn't stop laughing. James never mentioned the day Abe cried again. He hadn't even thought about it until now.

Abe looked the same, with his head pressed against Elise's body, his cheek pressed against her white shirt, like her cheek had pressed against the white sheet, his tears streaming down until absorbed by her clothes as they both sat in the puddle of blood.

"Help him lift her up," James said. Tic-Tac and Shia hovered over Abe. They bent to help him lift Elise to the bed. James had gotten them instead of the boys designated to be peacekeepers and transporters. He didn't want to alarm the settlement.

Tic-Tac and Shia were part of the committee and knew how to keep quiet.

"No," Abe said. "No! Stop it! Don't touch her!" He didn't let go of her. Shia pulled Abe back. His hands were wrapped around Elise. Her body was flaccid and heavy. His arms loosened. He let go. Elise's body fell to the floor. The blood sprayed across the side of the room, against Abe's face, against the sheets. Bits of blood splashed across Tic-Tac from his knees down. He bent over and brought her to the bed. The sheet absorbed the blood painted on her back.

"A knife," Abe said. "Why was that out of the kitchen? A goddamned knife!" Shia held Abe.

When Elise and James had talked in the kitchen, all she had wanted was her initials carved next to Abe's. James had never imagined that this would happen. His heart raced. Sweat poured down his face. Did Abe notice?

James couldn't catch his breath. He had allowed Elise to leave the kitchen with the knife.

"How could she do this?" James whispered. *It isn't my fault*, he told himself.

The more Abe screamed, the harder it was for James to convince himself that he couldn't have known what Elise would have done with the knife; he never could have stopped her.

James wanted to hug his friend, to hug Elise, to find a way to bring it all back together. He stood this close to death when Marcus had been torn apart, but James hadn't seen it. James had known Elise since he was eleven years old, and he was as helpless and useless at protecting her from herself as he was at protecting Marcus from a feral pack of scavs.

"A goddamn knife!" Abe screamed.

James wrapped his arms around Abe. James's body shook. His stomach roiled. The words took shape in his mouth. He wanted to say it was his fault. He'd allowed Elise to leave with the knife. He swallowed the bitter words and stayed silent.

EMPTY SPACES

JAMES

THE MOON LINGERED OVER THE FOREST WITH A COLD, WIDE eye, and James found himself without a coat. How long it would it take him to freeze? The lingering cough strangled his lungs. *What if tomorrow brings warm sun?*

Cuddled up in the warmth of his bed, where the steam seeped through the pipes on purpose to keep the settlement warm and alive without having to defrost their eyelashes every day—every minute, even—James thought about the day Marcus died, the day Robert died, and now the day Elise died. All the days had one thing in common: the cold. James had believed the cold brought destruction.

Then he realized what else all three deaths had in common—people shrouded by fear and undelivered promises. They were all the same, in some way, James thought, all torn apart.

He daydreamed about a body with bound wrists tied to a pillar; the strain of the rope rubbed against the skin and slowly tore it away to the muscle, the pink skin ripping apart until the tendons showed. A screaming eagle circled, crying out like the whistling wind. It swooped down every chance it had, ransacking the regenerating liver of the lifeless corpse—a limitless food supply borne by death.

The settlement was now a series of organs that reproduced themselves in a non-living thing. At least Marcus didn't make it, Robert tried to run away, and Elise had the sense to end it. Abe huddled over her body like a lost puppy searching its mother's dead body for milk, hidden somewhere he couldn't reach. James started to worry.

The committee had called a meeting to figure out what to do with Elise's body. Too often they had been faced with the fact of having to fill a need they preferred to avoid. They weren't naive enough to think no one would die in the settlement, but they were hopeful enough to think it wouldn't come for a long time. A kid who died in the dome was disgraced, unworthy of a burial. They were supposed to be forgotten and disposed of without ceremony, so they were dropped into a hole carved out of thin ice, given back to the elements that helped shape the settlement. Elise was the first to die outside of the dome, but she wouldn't be the last, no matter how much James wished. The committee needed to decide how to honor the dead, not just dispose of the dishonored.

Abe wasn't allowed into the meeting. James wouldn't let him in. Tic-Tac said he would babysit Abe. There were too many questions that needed to be answered and discussed of which Abe shouldn't take part. James told himself it was necessary, for Abe and for the committee, to make sure the best decisions were made for everyone and the settlement's future. But James admitted silently that he didn't trust Abe, not with Elise's death, not with Robert's death, and not with death at all.

Tic-Tac said that Abe had stayed with Elise with his hands wrapped around her the entire time the committee met.

"It was weird and . . . I don't know, just weird," Tic-Tac said. "Tragic even. He pressed his head to her chest the entire time. He rocked her back and forth like a . . . a baby or something. It looked crazy.

"How'd she look?" Charlotte asked.

The pressure caught up to Abe and broke him, James thought. *It was only a matter of time.*

"She looked like when we first found her," Tic-Tac said.

"I wasn't there," Charlotte said.

"What does it matter?" James asked. "She's dead."

"She looked peaceful," Tic-Tac said with a serene touch to his voice.

"Things matter, James," Charlotte said. "Even if they don't matter to you."

Abe sat with Elise in their bed. Soon all traces of her would be gone. His body sunk into the mattress with the weight of feeling alone for the first time. Maybe Abe wouldn't be alone forever but James knew he was alone for now.

The committee met in secret. They didn't want panic to wash over the settlement; they wouldn't be able to calm everyone once panic took over. They all knew the rules and the rules stated that, at least with silverware, someone needed to be punished. No one was above the rules, and now the person with the silverware was already dead. Would someone still need to be punished? First the committee needed to figure out how, where, and when to bury Elise.

"Bury her," Charlotte had said. "It's the most humane way."

"Burn her," Shia said. "It's just better for everyone. Where can we bury her?"

"Sink her," Sarah said. "It gets the body far away and we don't have to worry about digging."

James didn't like the idea of digging. It's not that he couldn't dig. A hole didn't scare him, but every time he put a shovel to the ground he couldn't help but think back to the moment the ice cracked and he fell into the drink, almost drowned, and would have been shit out of luck if it hadn't been for Tic-Tac.

The committee ruled out the fire because it sounded too barbaric, and James didn't think Elise's body would burn consistently and thoroughly enough once they took away her clothing. The settlement couldn't waste that much wood on a single burial.

"Have you ever smelled burnt hair?" James asked. "You can't run away from that. It sticks in your mind like a toothache, even when you think you wash it away."

James had smelled it once when Abe and he pretended to be firemen. They had seen smoke from a distance and ran five blocks to the fire. The smoke cluttered the sky. The fire trucks were out front, lights flashing, surrounded by big men in yellow gear smeared with ash. Fire hoses pulsed off and on. The water smashed against the house. The air reeked of burnt wood and melted glass, until a fire-fighter came out with a child in his arms. Her head was tilted over the fireman's arm, lifeless. Her arms were limp in the air. The fireman pulled his helmet off and placed the girl on the concrete sidewalk. Ash covered her skin like she had been wrapped in smoke.

The man pressed his hands—big, gloved hands—to the girl's chest. He pushed and pressed and pushed and pressed, and the world looked, for a second, to surround him, to surround Abe and James and the girl who could have been just younger than them. Her hair sprawled on the concrete like leaking water reaching for the drain. The fireman told her to breathe. Yelled at her to breathe, but she didn't move. Her chest pulsed when the man pressed into it, the only movement she made. The smell of charred wood left and the girl's hair continued to smolder. Then James smelled it, the burnt hair smell, petrol and fresh vomit—acidic. That's when James learned what that smell was, the living despair of hope dying.

"We can't sink her," Charlotte said. "Bodies float and we have nothing we can attach her to."

"A rock," Sarah said. "Tie her up and let her go."

"That seems a little too cavalier," James said.

"I didn't mean it like—"

"This is a precedent," Charlotte said.

"A press-a—?" Shia asked.

"A precedent," Charlotte said. "This is the way it'll work for everyone after this moment. Do we have that many rocks? Do we have that much material to wrap around everyone we need to do this for?"

It was a question no one wanted to ask but a good thing someone had. It was a moment that would define the rest of the settlement and how they reacted and worked. If they ran out of rope or string or material to tie to people's bodies then how would they progress? They couldn't hold onto a body in town; that's when diseases spread. And closure would be unobtainable, not that most of these kids knew much about closure anyway.

"I think burying her is our best bet," James said, despite how he felt about the shovels and axes. It was the best way to dispose of someone they cared about and the best way for them all to grieve.

It was the first decision of many. They decided the grave needed to be dug before they walked to the forest. They decided Elise should be stripped and cleaned and dressed in deerskin. The animal and its pelt had become revered as a new source of life, feeding and blanketing the settlement. As much as James wanted to pretend that the cleaning was ceremonial, it was more of a reason to strip Elise of her clothes without people thinking it lewd and callow. They would take her clothes, wash them, and give them to someone else, not because they were heartless, but because they hadn't figured out a way to produce clothes. The deer could make a coat, a wrap, or a blanket, but they couldn't make clothes. At least no one knew how yet. The committee wanted someone close to her, after the washing, to ferry the body to the gravesite on the trolley the settlement had taken from the cruise ship, and place her body into the earth. People could help if asked, but only by the carrier, whose charge it would be to ensure the body made it safely to rest. This would become their tradition.

The settlement stood at the edge of the forest where James had watched the wild dogs attack a deer when they first arrived on the island. Not many people ventured into the woods, mostly the hunters and the kids that dared one another to do so, calling each other cowards if they didn't take three steps deeper into the forest. The dogs were another fear that ran through the worries of the island. The committee hadn't made the forest off limits yet, but they often spoke of it.

Abe walked with Elise in his arms, her body blue except for where her wrists were stretched open by the knife. They never had time to scab over before her heart stopped. Abe held her like the fireman had held the little girl. Elise's hair draped from her head and flowed like water before all the water had frozen over, serene. Her body looked different but her lips were hers, the one part of her James remembered because of how long she had spent behind her parka where he could see only her eyes and her lips.

James wouldn't have been able to tell who a person was until he blocked out their surrounding features and focused on what he had seen over and over again—their eyes and nose and mouth. Elise was no different except that he had known her longer. Her body had changed over the years. It was her eyes that made James shiver, not the cold. Her eyes weren't the eyes he knew from San Diego, even from within the border of her parka hood. They were closed now but when they had been open, her eyes, once hazel, were washed with a white-blue, the same as the landscape. Somehow, even after death, her lips stayed pink and pouty. Even though she slid the knife against her own wrist, maybe she didn't want to die.

Abe set Elise on the table they had placed before the grave. Her hair ran over the edges and dripped into the air. He kissed his fingers, placed them on her lips, and stood beside her. Charlotte kissed her fingers, placed them on Elise's lips, and walked away. James did the same. And onward it went, each person saying goodbye to a friend, a chieftess, a mentor, a person they had seen but never met, or a person they had met but never knew. This was the settlement, once a part of Fornland and home to Elise; this was death; this was life; and the air was cold against the trees. When the last person pressed her fingers to Elise's lips, Abe scooped up her body and lowered her onto a bed of crisscrossed ropes. Four boys used the ropes to lay Elise in her grave.

They covered her body with soil they had unfrozen with warm water. They had first collected the snow and melted it down, poured the water on the soil to thaw it, shoveled the mud aside, and gave themselves enough time to break deep enough into the earth for a proper grave. It may not have been as easy as setting a fire or sinking beneath the ocean, but it was better. At some point James wanted to wrap himself in the cold air and join her, just to be done with what the world had become.

Charlotte wrapped her arms around James. He wasn't sure if anyone cried. Elise's body faded away one push of snowy dirt at a time. James coughed and nestled into Charlotte's arms. Everyone watched the hole fill in. Sometime, in the time gone by, they had all reached out and collected one another's hands, clenching tightly to one another as the community lessened by one. This was what Fornland had become. This was what James had become. Abe hadn't refused to let anyone help with the dirt—this was what Abe had become.

LOST TIME, NOT FORGOTTEN

ABE

I'M GIVING UP ON YOU, CAME AND WENT THROUGH ABE'S head a tumult of times, like an avalanche of worries and doubts that cascaded over him, leaving him covered in snow. He had placed Elise at the bottom of the hole and kissed her lips with his fingers, not because he was supposed to but because he couldn't imagine kissing her lips with his lips with her wrists fresh and open.

In a cold world filled with more questions than answers and too many frozen tears, there had been too much stuffed between them for him to break through and kiss her with his lips. The only way he thought he could have touched her was with his fingers—his fingers to his lips, his fingers to her lips, pushing away all the unsaid bullshit stuffed between them—so he could say goodbye. Now he felt more like a coward than a hero, unlike the firemen he had idolized and more like the boy who had stood frozen on the San Diego shore and watched his best friend fall into the ocean.

There was a time when their initials graced the concrete on a sidewalk in San Diego. They'd come too far from that moment when the cement was wet and the ground was visible. If there were a moment that Abe wished he could run from, it would be this moment. There was a time Abe believed that if he lost everything, he would have nothing left to worry about. With Elise gone he felt that he *had* finally lost everything. It didn't make life feel lighter. The world still felt as heavy as it had before Elise died. It felt even heavier now that Elise was gone. *Losing everything doesn't mean there is nothing left to lose,* Abe thought, and now understood.

He whispered into the corners of his empty

room, empty without Elise and filled with the scent of decomposing mint and basil. He felt so small in the world that was too inconsistent with life to understand what it meant to live, in the snow, in the woods, as some sort of guide for kids who didn't know where to step. He hadn't known where to step and could have fallen through the ice.

He wanted to sit in the hole with Elise and not let go. He hadn't let go of her body after he found her on the bed, dyeing the sheets with her blood. He didn't know how long he had pressed his face into her chest. If he sat there and pressed hard enough he thought he could fill her veins with saltwater and she'd come back, maybe even jump into the sea and be healed, in the way that they had all been shaped and formed by the sea. Too much had gone already, even in the way he wanted to kiss her lips before he laid her down but couldn't.

When they were twelve, it was easy to think they would last as long as their initials would, molded in concrete, which meant forever. The whole point of concrete was that it lasted, firm in the ground, and if not forever they would wait until the next time they found wet concrete and write their initials in the San Diego ground all over again.

"It's like having an address," Elise had said.

There was always a moment when any Fornland kid realized things weren't forever, that even when they found a glint of happiness, it might not last. Abe knew that that was Elise's moment. Parents left, friends left, the seasons changed, even in San Diego, but sometimes they could carve out a decent enough life for themselves amidst the changing landscape to be happy for a minute. The hard part was watching that minute come due; the clock ticked the last seconds away and they were stuck with the empty hole in their stomachs that wouldn't stop growing until they made that minute happen again.

Abe wouldn't make that same mistake now. He stepped out into the snow in front of his door where everyone could see, not hidden against the forest's edge, to mark where Elise's body was buried. Her body was only a part of her, while the rest of her was hiding in Abe's memories, and always would, in the last touch of his fingers to her lips, the way her body felt weightless in his arms, the way her hair draped over the table like a waterfall, the way she just wanted to know he loved her.

Abe didn't put on a coat or shoes or socks or a hat. He opened his door and watched the steam pour into the air. His feet stuck to the snow. The cold pricked his skin. He dug his finger into the white and carved Æ as large as he could until his finger was numb and he thought he could break off the tip of it with a snap.

He looked over the letters and carved another pair of initials next to the first set. He used the same finger. The numbness spread beneath his skin, through the muscle. His finger started to pale. He didn't notice the pins and needles pricking his limbs, tingling his arms. He watched the absence of color sprawl across his fingertip, creeping around his fingernail, fat shrinking, muscles losing oxygen. He should have pressed his hands beneath his armpit to stop the frostbite from spreading. Instead he walked back into his room and closed the door. Heat overtook the room. His finger stayed numb. The steam disappeared. The letters stayed for the moment.

UNAVOIDABLE LIFE

JAMES

JAMES STOOD IN THE COMMITTEE ROOM WHERE AN EMPTY chair sat at the table. Abe's eyes had black burrows beneath them since he took his face away from Elise's chest.

Today the committee came together to try and find Elise's replacement. They needed to discuss their options. Voices outside the doors demanded Geoff be placed on the committee, as he had wanted in the first place. With Elise's death, people started to question if the committee was fit to lead. As if Abe didn't hurt enough, now he had to worry about the settlement not trusting his leadership decisions because he didn't see Elise's death coming.

It reminded James of the snowstorm that brought them all to the island and the moment they all could have done something but didn't. It's not as though the rest of the settlement's members hadn't thought about a knife to their own wrists or keeping their heads beneath the hot springs until they wouldn't be able to come up for air. People stopped worrying about drowning in the frozen sea after James and Tic-Tac survived. *Something about the after-effects of failed death turns people off to the possibilities*, James thought. Suicidal thoughts came with seclusion and an eternal winter. There was some statistic before it all went to shit that Scandinavian countries were the happiest in the world but also had the highest suicide rate. Depression could come out of the trees like a rabid dog and attack somewhere between the snow, the lack of sun, and the empty darkness that crept into everyone. He didn't blame Elise; he only wished he could have helped. No matter how hard he tried, it was never help enough.

"Maybe we should just bring in Geoff," Shia said. "So many people think he should have been on the committee from the start."

"It's not about what they think," Tic-Tac said. "It's about what's best for them."

Tic-Tac had seen the possibility of awful in the world, the type of disgust that brought most people to the brink of insanity, where they'd rather bury their heads in the sand or bury a knife into their wrists than be haunted by what the world could do to itself. It never seemed like Tic-Tac was affected. His cough had gone; James's cough had stayed. When Tic-Tac's cough had disappeared so did his penchant for optimism.

"It's realism," Tic-Tac said.

Realism is a word created by pessimists to show that their way of thinking isn't fatalistic, the world is, James thought.

"Sometimes I have to remind myself that not all stories end happily," Tic-Tac said.

"There are those that do," Charlotte had said. It was after Elise's funeral. James hadn't noticed at the time that Elise's blood still stained Tic-Tac's hands with a rough red that refused to leave. He either hadn't washed or didn't wash hard enough. Part of James believed the color on Tic-Tac's skin was a collection of all the blood that had been around recently and Tic-Tac had unintentionally witnessed: the ice, the glass in Claire's eye, the pool of blood beneath Elise. There had to be a time when all the bodies and possibilities blended together to make some complete smiling mess that absorbed him. Sarah stood in the corner and watched the conversation but didn't say a word. Maybe Charlotte had been right. Maybe Tic-Tac and Sarah had drifted apart and James wasn't clued in enough to notice, to see how his friend may have needed him in the midst of the cracks of their community. Even though their settlement was up and running, too much of their nature had broken apart.

"I wanted to say something," Tic-Tac said. "I didn't know how." Sarah looked more angry than concerned, as if she were hurt most from Tic-Tac's silence. Her arms were crossed. Tic-Tac stared at the table.

"It's okay to be upset," Charlotte said. "We've all seen stuff we would rather forget." Some nights James would wake up helpless as Charlotte screamed from the image of her parents crunched beneath a Land Rover while searching for her. It was the same nightmare each time. Her parents slow down in the darkness to look into the shadows of a park. They think they see a silhouette of their daughter somewhere on the benches, then the Land Rover hits them from the side, her mom's head smashes the window, her dad's head cracks against the wheel, and the car folds in on itself without even a hint of their daughter in the background. *Sometimes it is the nightmares of what we haven't seen that are worse*, James thought. He coughed so hard he spat blood sometimes. *Other times there is just too much we would all rather forget.*

"We're supposed to be here to help," Sarah said. "We're supposed to do what's best for the settlement. That includes us." She grabbed Tic-Tac's hand. James wasn't sure if what she said agreed with his point or if she wanted to reassure Tic-Tac. It was a simple touch but it whipped the realistic look from Tic-Tac's face. He needed to believe in the warmth of Sarah's skin wrapped over his, something honest and tangible.

Abe didn't pay attention. His usual playfulness was absent, gone. He stared at the table with empty eyes, his hand cupped over his mouth. It looked like it was all that kept his head attached.

"There's other people to look—" James said.

"Where's Geoff?" Abe asked. "I don't care— bring him here."

Geoff had been outside. He was supposed to

be somewhere working; everyone was supposed to work. It took all their minds off of what they didn't have and what they didn't know. Geoff could have been held for that, but not today. He stood in the center of the room. There was a small look of uncertainty at the corner of his lips where James thought he could call out most people's bull. Eyes could lie, but lips couldn't.

"You want to be on the committee?" Abe asked.

"It think there is good reason," Geoff said, "to broaden the type of people on—"

"Find out where Elise got the knife," Abe said. "Do that and you're in."

"That isn't part of the ru—" James said.

"This is our rule now," Abe said. "She got that knife from somewhere and I want to know from where. You bring me proof of that, Geoff, and her spot is your spot."

"Wasn't she punished enough?" Tic-Tac asked.

"Who said anything about punishment?" Abe asked. "We're being punished, the rest of us, because someone disobeyed the rules. This is what happens when you don't listen."

It wasn't silence that snuck around the room, but a variety of breaths. James heard each exhale as a statement of fear, excitement, anger, and uncertainty. Everyone breathed at a different rate that told him, without words or acknowledgement, how they felt about Abe's last sentence—his last decree. Sarah breathed the slow breaths of incomprehension; Shia held his breath in fear; Geoff's were excited and deep. Charlotte's breaths were shallow, borne of concern; she turned away from everyone and looked absently at the floor. Abe breathed in anger, the strict exhalation of vengeance, looking for someone to blame when no one was at fault. James knew he breathed but he couldn't hear or feel or see his breath in the room. There was a line between grief and friendship, leadership and fear, that no one wanted to cross. Someone had to cross the line.

"What if it was her?" James asked. James felt himself breathe again. It was hot against his chest.

He wanted to cough but tried to hold it in. The cough would make it look like he spoke out of turn. He felt everyone's eyes on him. They batted at him like batons, each eye a hit against his ribs, back, face; he wanted to shield himself more from their looks than from Abe's reaction.

"What does that mean?" Abe asked.

"It's an 'if,' Abe. What *if* she took the knife herself?"

"You don't think someone would have said something? You don't think someone would have reported that to me or you or them?" He stood up, smacked the table, and pointed at the committee.

"No," James said. "I don't. For the same reason they wouldn't if one of us took it." James hadn't said anything because part of him forgot she had taken it, another part of him wanted to forget.

"Geoff," Abe said. "Find out."

The uncertainty in Geoff's lips turned into a smirk. It didn't matter who Geoff pointed out. If the committee couldn't convince Abe to call off the search it would become a witch-hunt. Geoff knew that. He could point to anyone, other than Abe, with some sideward-glanced certainty, without needing more than a false witness he could drum up from somewhere. No one wanted to be the face where the finger fell when Geoff finished pointing.

"Play the part and play safe," Abe had told James when they had stood in the record store. The cops had come. James followed Abe's lead. They acted like the store clerks that had arrived at the break-in first. They played the part, played it safe, and walked out without cuffs on. When shit hits the fan, get out of the fan's way so you don't get sprayed with what was left. James stepped into the wind and was about to get hit with all the shit that blew back.

"Count on it," Geoff said. He walked out of the committee.

"You said he'll need proof," Charlotte said. "What proof could he possibly get? What proof could anyone possibly get?"

"Someone out there knows," Abe said.

"Put him on the committee," Tic-Tac said. "But don't put him on the hunt. It won't do anything. It won't mean anything."

"It means everything," Abe said.

Abe spoke the last words of the meeting.

NIGHTMARES AREN'T IN YOUR HEAD

JAMES

THE MORNING GRAY WASHED THROUGH THE WINDOW OF James's room. The night before he had stayed awake with Charlotte while her nightmare kept her up and frightened for a while. Charlotte rocked back and forth with her knees to her chest, the sheets pushed off of the bed, James's hand pressed to her back over and over again to remind her he was there. It was a process that he had become somewhat used to. She would burst awake in frantic gasps. The sheets would fly off. The white tips of her hair would flash and twirl like the tail end of an avalanche. She would bite down on the palms of her hands to keep herself from screaming. It was a sad luxury that James couldn't remember his parents; the last person that came close to that type of connection was Bernice, who had her own family and her own concerns beyond Fornland and beyond James.

The first time Charlotte jumped awake, James had tried to hug her, but she shouldered him in the mouth, and gave him a bloody lip. He learned. He would rub her back, his hand moving up and down the length of her spine, where he could almost feel every tick and click of each vertebrae. She would shrug him away. The longer he did it the more he soothed her. Maybe she just fought less, but she would calm down, roll into James's arms and, sometimes, fall asleep. Other times she would stay awake, looking out at the walls in silence. James counted her breaths, listening to the repetition, knowing that it was too consistent to be real sleep, too contrived to make him think she fell into peaceful rest. She would give in, but they both knew she was awake.

Sometimes people didn't want to talk; sometimes it was the silences that brought them closer together.

"What do you think is going to happen with Abe?" Charlotte asked.

"I think there's no snow tonight," James said. "Looks quiet outside."

"I mean it," Charlotte said. "We all have snow shoveled over our pasts, some part of us covered in this shit. Why is this different?"

"He's always approached his problems differently," James said. "He was almost adopted once."

"Everyone knows that," she said. She maneuvered herself closer into James's body. "How he turned down leaving Fornland. It sounds like a bunch of bullshit I don't need to hear."

"That would be," James said. "It didn't happen like that." James could feel the heat of her body. "They liked him. They just didn't want to wait for the adoption period. It took its toll on him; we had thought we were immune to that kind of fallout.

It was kind of that moment we realized we weren't invincible. At least I did."

"Who started the rumor that he turned them down?"

"Not his style. Sounds more like Geoff. We never talked about it again. That was how we worked; that's how Abe works. Except . . . "

James kissed Charlotte's shoulder. She turned to face him. Her hair lay on the pillow like a mixture of warm snow and burnt oak. She pressed her nose to his, so close her eyes blurred into one.

"Except," she said.

"All these other things faded away," James said. "They were easy enough to run away from in one way or another. You see the initials he put in the snow? He's been doing it every day with his bare hands, over and over again since Elise's funeral. I think a part of him thinks if he had taken the time to mark their initials, she wouldn't have done it. Not that it'll bring her back, but—

"It would have helped," Charlotte said.

"What?" James said.

"It would have," Charlotte said. "If Abe had taken the time to carve their initials. It would have been some small show of affection; something that showed a piece of him was still hers. She needed comfort, James, from anyone."

"She told me," James said. "Sort of."

"When?" Charlotte asked.

"When I went to tell Abe about Buck and Rudy. She asked me if I noticed anything missing."

"By then it wasn't just about the initials, I'm sure."

"She had said . . . it was," James stifled a cough. "It was just easier knowing these things would go away, that we could run away from them. There's nowhere else to run."

"I don't see how running ever worked."

"It didn't," James said. "In the end you just get tired and it all catches up."

The conversation in the dark hours of the morning had shifted by sunrise. In the silence before dawn, James always felt like his secrets were cloaked in the darkness. By the time the sun rose and the light showed, it burned away all the night's whispers. James felt that the longer they stayed on the island, the more muffled conversations wandered around in the snow, leaving tracks in the woods, never burning, never fading, always ready to return and haunt James in the future.

The chair lay quiet on its side. Its wooden legs reached out to the side in an unnatural way, when the chair was meant to sit up, to look forward and straight. The bed sheets were tangled and torn. The air rose through the floor and sat warm and heavy over the room. The air never changed in the room, not before and not after. Pieces from the ship had decorated the space, splayed around in a recreation of how James and Charlotte had decided a personalized room should look, where they placed picture frames on the table next to the bed, even though they had no photos inside them. A mirror had hung over the far side of the room. Now it lay on the floor, cracked and devastated. The sound of crunched glass had lingered thick like the snow they all stepped on outside, over and over and over again, but James hadn't heard the glass break over the shrill of tormented screams. The high-pitched terror of Charlotte's voice played on repeat in his mind. He couldn't get it out of his thoughts—the image of her fighting the guards that had come to take him away in the slow gray of dawn. The screen had a hole in it, pushed over onto the floor leaning against the bed like a ramp to the corners of their torn paradise in the snow. The guards had pushed her against the wall, against the mirror, her head rammed into the glass. The first crack James heard. The beads of blood from the side of her head smeared, streaked, and reflected in the shards. The kids burst in and the cold forced its way through the open door. They grabbed James. He tried to keep calm, let himself drift away—until they pushed Charlotte.

They held her there as she screamed, "Let me go! Let him go! What the fuck are you doing?" Her usual pragmatism broken like the mirror. The second crack, the mirror fell. The third crack, the shatter.

James tried to fight the guards. Images of his own bloody face pressed against the kitchen floor in Fornland passed through his mind. He threw elbows in the air. He kicked and hoped he hit someone but caught empty spaces. He shut his eyes to block out the frozen memory of the last fight he had, with Kevin Summers, when Kevin split open James's face and left him on the cement kitchen floor.

The harder James closed his eyes, the more the memory taunted him beneath Charlotte's angry calls for help. The guards punched James in the stomach, kicked him in the back of the knees, and dragged him, half naked, out of his room, and away from Charlotte.

James was in the committee room. Abe sat at the head of the table, his face filled with the same faraway look held so often, where his eyes didn't focus, just stared off into somewhere no one else could see, and his hand wrapped around his mouth to hide some silent cry no one else could hear. Geoff stood next to James, a stupid grin hidden at the side of his lips. James stood with his hands in front of him. The fight he had tried to put up wasn't for himself but for Charlotte. Her screams continued to rattle in his head. She wasn't in the room. He didn't know where she was.

"How could you?" Abe asked.

"You could have called me," James said. "You didn't have to drag me out like a dead deer."

Geoff stayed silent, the stupid grin stuck to his stupid face.

"Why would you?" Abe asked. "She was your friend. She was my wife."

"She was—what?"

Abe stood up. His voice was low. James had to lean forward to hear it.

"You gave Elise the knife."

"I gave Elise the knife?"

"He confessed," Geoff said.

"You shut your goddamn mouth, Geoff," James said. "Where the hell did this idea come from—your wife?"

"You practically said it in the committee meeting," Geoff said. "No one would have pointed a finger at someone on the committee. You were begging to be caught."

"Call her what you want," Abe said. "She's dead and it's your fault."

"You didn't do much to keep her alive."

"What's that mean?" Abe yelled. He motioned to the guards who then punched James in the stomach once more. The force caused him to cough. The tension in his guts and lungs engulfed him. *This is what it feels like to suffocate*, James thought.

"What the fuck does that mean?"

"How's your finger?" James ignored his breath-lessness.

"She was your friend," Abe said. Blistered red skin bordered Abe's fingertip. James didn't know much about medicine, but if Abe didn't take care of that finger it looked like he could lose his entire hand. He had spent too much time digging his finger into the snow; it was frostbitten. Sooner or later it would start to smell more rancid than the stink of the settlement before Abe allowed deodorant. That finger would always remind Abe of his failure to protect Elise, James knew. Abe tried to hide his finger from James, even now. If anyone was at fault, it was Abe.

"I didn't kill her," James said. "You ever think she wanted out?" James coughed and doubled over. It burned through his lungs until his mouth filled with mucus and he spat blood.

"Out of what?" Abe screamed over James's cough. "This life? This is how we live, and we were kings!"

144

"You were king," James said. "And this piece of shit doesn't know what he's talking about. I didn't break any rules."

"Is this a dispute then?" Abe asked.

"It sounds like one," Geoff said. He didn't hide the twisted joy in the back of his voice.

"You're goddamned right it is," James said. "Geoff, what are you doing? You know what this means. Why would you even try this?"

"You're guilty," Geoff said. "That's why."

"Then the argument must be settled," Abe said. "Tomorrow. Some sort of justice will be done."

"Tomorrow," Geoff said.

"This isn't justice," James said. "This is revenge, retribution. You're trying to fight something that can't be fought, Abe. She killed herself. You can't fight that. You made the rules to keep people from doing that even if they could. Revenge solves nothing."

"This isn't revenge, James." Abe never called James by his name. He always called James

"Hamez." It had become a term of endearment between Abe and James. The darkness fell on James with his name, the way a parent uses a child's full name when in trouble, and James realized that this wouldn't end early and it wouldn't end pretty. "We're following the rules."

"Where's the proof?" James asked. "Where's the proof that I gave her the knife?"

"We have a witness," Geoff said.

"Who?"

"Him," Geoff said. A shadow hovered in the corner. Small, a corral, or close to one. He tried to creep deeper into the darkness. "He asked who; now come out and show him."

Shia stepped into the light. He didn't look at James. He didn't look at anyone. His stare was cast so far into the ground he tried to dig a hole with his eyes.

"That can't be right," James said.

"Tomorrow, you and Geoff," Abe said. "Into the Icedome."

Two kids grabbed James's arms and started to drag him away.

"That can't be right!" James said. "Shia?" Then James remembered Shia in the kitchen when Elise took the knife and James said nothing.

The light from the door came into view. Shia once again became a shadow. Before James was pushed out into the snow he looked back, saw Shia's face, his eyes, the corners of his lips, and thought he whispered, "I'm sorry."

COUNTING SECONDS

ABE

JAMES WOULD NOT LAST MUCH LONGER. A SMALL TEAR opened in Abe's heart for the things he couldn't control and how much he wished he could. If he could have slept with the awful fright that kept him up at night, he wouldn't rise and shine with the screams that now got caught in his throat. Sometimes he dreamed he gulped pints of Elise's blood as it flowed out of her wrists, warm and thick like some viscous water, melted snow, pungent putrescence. He would spring awake at the sound of a disembodied voice in the back of his mind telling him to smile, as if that would change his life or how he felt.

Elise was dead and James would join her soon.

There was no doubt about it. The last fight James had ever been in was when he got his head smashed into the concrete at Fornland. There wasn't much to remember from San Diego, at least not much Abe wanted to remember, but no matter how much he tried to forget, how much he tried to replace his past with stories James had told, certain parts of Abe's life would never be forgotten. People always said "It was for the best." The best wasn't good enough when all he wanted to do was move on.

That morning Abe had stood at the gates of Icedome. What fucked up world did they live in when the things they valued most revolved around a dome made of ice that looked like a circular cell, which was all it was. "Do whatever just to stay alive." It became the motto that overtook the world when the snow fell. Abe refused to live by that life now; he hadn't wanted to live by that idea then. *Sometimes you just don't have a choice.* Somewhere along the line he lost the effortlessness of wearing a coat, when the weight didn't bother him as much and he could stand out in the snow with three layers or more on his shoulders and not feel weighed down. Since the ship and the construction of their little village, their settlement, their new Fornland, he hadn't had to wear a coat much, only when he needed to step outside. The coat brought him more comfort now than it ever had before; wrapped around his shoulders, it gave him what he no longer had—something to hold against his body.

When his mother died and his dad was on the verge of death with the whites of his eyes rolling into red, Abe remembered how they leaned against one another—another moment of his life he didn't understand why he remembered and would rather replace with some story about why the sky sparkled at night or why the snow stuck to his skin, whether true or not. He couldn't take the rumble in his head that whispered James's name over and over again, within the confluence of events that took Elise and his best friend away in one fell swoop. One event, two losses, like another shot of shit straight to his parents' veins that left them lifeless in Abe's life.

Abe swung open the jailhouse door and brought the breeze in through the doorframe. "We could have changed everything," Abe said. Remnants of ice crusted along the outer walls of the door and flaked inside. They turned to water and dripped to the floor. He didn't close the door. "We had almost changed everything. We were right there. Things were ours and you went and fucked it all up!"

"You're right," James said. James squinted when the wind hit his face. His shoes were gone and his coat was lying over the empty space where a mattress should have been. Abe closed the door. He took off his coat.

"That's it?"

"Things have changed," James said.

"This whole thing was ours. Why would you go and do something like that? You know we can't change the rules."

"Why can't we?" James asked.

"Because I said so," Abe said. A simple flash of words brought Abe back to the memory of his father beating up another father, telling Abe to punch the child, proving Abe was a *man*, and could defend his family name, a name no one even cared about anymore.

Abe sat down on his coat. He pulled at his hair. There was too much he wanted to spit at James and couldn't think of where to start. Too much tore at them both, but mostly the fact that James didn't just break a rule, Elise died because of it. There was no reason for either of them to be in this position—for Elise to be dead, for James to be on the brink of death, or for Abe to stand and watch his best friend die. Who was going to carry James to the edge of the forest?

"I won't get to the graveyard," James said. They'd known each other long enough to know what the other was thinking, to some degree. Abe never tried to hide it, not from James. The Icedome was a trial of virtue. You lost, you died; if you died, it meant you didn't get a proper burial. The loser got thrown away, trashed like the world they once lived in. Everyone ran from you and left you there to die alone—even though you'd already died. It was the caretaker's job to get rid of the body. The only people who knew what was done with the losers were Abe and James; no one else wanted a part in it.

"We do what we need to, to stay alive," Charlotte had said. "That's good enough for me." The others had agreed but it meant they preferred to keep some of their humanity intact—they didn't want to know what decrepit way was needed to get rid of the lifeless bodies taken away from the torrential white snow.

"Somewhere there is a floating graveyard that's coming for us," James said. "I guess it'll just find me first." The caretaker, Mo (short for Mohammad), was one of the older kids at Fornland but still a newbie when the snow started to fall. He hadn't had enough time to make friends among the misfits.

In the end it didn't seem like he wanted to. He was stocky for a fifteen-year-old.

He was at school when his parents were torn apart by some anti-Muslim protestors that claimed they had been threatened or felt threatened or thought they saw an unattended bag somewhere near Mo's parents. The rest of his family had lived in London. His parents weren't even from the Middle East, they were from northern India, but geography and understanding never mattered when fear was enough of a motivator to drive action. There went Mo's parents, and there Mo went to Fornland.

"How long you in for?" Abe had asked Mo.

"Not long," Mo said.

"It means 'how old are you?'" Abe said. "You're only here 'til you're eighteen. Then you're out."

"How would I have known that?" Mo asked.

"Okay," Abe said. "Then, how old are you?"

"It doesn't matter. I'm leaving soon."

"Everyone always is," Abe said.

It was only supposed to be until the government made arrangements for a flight to London. "Two weeks at most," Mo had said. The snow already fell; Europe was smothered in winter. Mo never boarded a plane. Abe assumed that Mo must have figured his family in England went the way of his parents, why else would he have tagged along with the cruise ship?

Mo had volunteered to work with the bodies. He did it in the dark of the night. He didn't squirm or fidget when they told him the plan. James had winced and coughed. He had feared the ice since he fell through it.

"Crack the ice," Abe had said. James couldn't say it to Mo, Abe knew, but it had been James's idea originally. *It's easy to forget that James is capable of some serious shit.* "That's it. Crack the ice and drop the body. The cold will eventually cover it up." According to Mo it had worked. That's how the unbearable cold worked, over the sea and over the dome: no matter how many cracks were made or how big the cracks were, once morning came the cold repaired the cracks, as if the snow worked like elves to patch up the earth. Only these patches everyone would rather see torn.

"I'll get better acquainted with Mo," James said. "I think it's about time."

"How can you just accept it all?" Abe asked. "How could you just go about it like this? She was mine to take care of. Of all the people to help pull her away—"

"It was her decision to make," James said. "Not mine. Not yours."

"Fuck you," Abe said.

"That's the end of it?" James asked. "That's all it comes down to."

"You remember that first story you told? There was a moment there when I started to believe you. That's what I thought and for a while I was able to forget about the rest of it."

"It's a lot harder to forget than to remember," James said.

"Those kids . . . all of the kids that had come to

Fornland, you had said, were rocks broken from the cliffs and shaped by the sea. Remember?"

"I wouldn't be able to forget."

"I wanted to believe that so much. I wanted to believe that we were shaped and carved from stone, that's what made us persistent and somewhat invincible. It's what made us survive in the hard times that just kept coming. Why do they just keep coming? We were shaped into children by the water and ended up at Fornland where the first boulder had ended up. It was a calling, 'fate,' you had said. That was our story. I believed in that story."

"It wasn't true. It isn't true."

"Who gives a shit if it's true? What about the story you told everyone about why the sun hides behind the clouds? You want them to go back to questioning why we had to run, or worse, remembering why? You remember that don't you? The way Marcus died?"

"You don't get to talk about that! You weren't there!"

"That's where you draw the line? Wouldn't you rather forget the way he died? Wouldn't you rather forget that he died at all? That's what you were giving all of us: a chance to forget that bad things happened. A chance to remember good things that might have happened if we just believed them long and hard enough. You told them, all those kids out there, what happened to Marcus. They believed you because they needed to. Then you told me the goddamned truth. Another thing you took away from me."

"You'd rather have the lie?"

"I'd rather have the choice!"

"Did you give Robert a choice?"

Abe took his shoe off and threw it at James. He wanted to hit him, spit in his face, do something, anything, but he couldn't even reach James through the gate. Abe took off his other shoe and threw it. The second throw hit James in the chest. Abe stood and started to pace the room. *Was that what it came down to? James betraying him and Elise and*

158

the settlement because of Captain? Abe ran his hands through his hair and turned to James. "Captain wasn't family!"

"That didn't give you the right to kill him."

"He wasn't what you thought he was. I was protecting you. I was protecting all of us."

"And you didn't give me the choice either," James said. "That was all it was. You took it and we all had to live with the consequences. What happens when our world starts to collapse? A fucking story can't replace the metal that's going to disintegrate or the clothes that'll tear. What happens then? Maybe Robert would have known."

"Maybe Captain would've taken over and remade another world like the one we ran from. You forget why we ran? He was the problem. Now he's gone. We made the rules; I lived by them."

"You made the rules."

"You don't get to back out of this one. You finally have to take responsibility for the shit you did, for the choices you were scared to make.

Welcome to the new world. This world means you face your shit and smell it."

"Some world," James said. "Black or white, live or die."

"Yes," Abe said. "And now you know."

James coughed. He laid back and Abe watched his chest heave. He rolled over and spit blood onto the floor. No matter how flush Abe felt, how bad he may have wanted to ask James if he was okay, or call for Rudy to check on James's lungs, he didn't. He stood and picked up his coat. He took off his socks and left them on the floor. Socks soaked up moisture and made his feet swell with cold. He never liked socks anyway.

"Hamez," Abe said. "This wasn't how it was supposed to be." Abe took out the book that he had hid under his clothes, the book James carried around since Marcus had died. Abe showed James.

"What are you doing with that?" James asked. "What are you doing?"

Abe tore out the pages and threw them onto

the hot pipe that led to the hot spring and brought the heat. His blotchy, blistered finger avoided the pages. The tear ripped at the quiet moment. James screamed and ran to the bars. He pressed his face against the metal and tried to force his way through. James's skin tightened and rubbed against the steel. His voice oscillated between high-pitched screams and brutal coughs. It looked like he tried to tear his skin off to fit through the bars.

Abe opened the door. A flurry twirled around his toes. The air was frost against his skin and the coat was heavy on his shoulders. He didn't think of the freeze or the jacket.

He didn't wait to hear what James had to say. They hadn't thought about what life away from San Diego would be like but Abe never thought it would be like this. The glossy pages melted into ash. James screamed in the empty room. There was a time when Abe would have questioned the rules at any cost. There was a time when Abe would have done a lot of things. Those times were gone. All they had left were the rules. Abe needed to follow them, not for James, not for his father, not for himself, but for the collection of kids that didn't know any better. The rules protected them all from floating beneath the cracks in the ice. *Elise would understand.* But Elise wasn't there.

IN AMONG THE BARS

JAMES

THERE WASN'T ANOTHER MOMENT THAT HE WOULD HAVE TO rise and shine, to stay awake with Charlotte for another minute as the sun blurred in some indistinct color that he thought he could see behind the gray that draped over the sky. The ice and the sky blended until the horizon disappeared, along with the world of which he was once a part.

"When it comes down to you and the world," James said, "who do you choose?" There was no one in the tiny room. Everyone had left him without shoes and without hope. Abe's shoes continued to sit on the floor. James could feel the melting snow and mud from the soles turning to slush on the ground.

Abe's shoes had left tracks on James's chest when he threw them yesterday. Night was the hardest to get through. The only person to talk to in the long stretch of darkness was himself, and he was also the only person to blame. On the hot pipe rested the ashes of Marcus's book, the only remnant of him left burned and disappeared, and all James could do was watch—again. James was stuck behind the bars and stiff in the warmth. He never wanted to be out in the cold so much, to dig his toes into the frost and let it freeze over his skin, turn his limbs black, maybe even get him stuck to the island's earth somewhere beneath the stretch of ice.

The old, the young, the brave, and the astounded swam around his mind as if he were the ocean and they were kids who came to visit. In the end though, as all oceans had, he froze and the kids turned their backs or they drowned, and no one ever came back to waters that couldn't be trusted.

James spent most of his time staring into the dark ceiling and hoping for a way out. He thought about how it would go, of the moments in his life that he had left.

Wake up. Eat breakfast. Get stripped by the guards. Get thrown into the dome where his challenger waited. Geoff would pounce on him. He would cough, double over, get hit, get grounded, get crunched, get punched, and in the end he would end up beneath the cracks of the ocean ice floating in a grave the water provided.

Kudos to him and the Fornlanders for this wonderful life they had created. This was the life James and Abe made, but it made James sick to think of the way they had come to the rules and the way Abe clung to them as though it would bring back a better time. Nostalgia was the only thing about their past that gave their lives any fondness. What could he hold on to?

James realized the only thing they had to hold on to wasn't their fake pasts or preferred present, it was each other, but that was gone now. That was what tore Abe apart in the end. The rules weren't to save and protect the settlement; the rules were meant to protect Abe and James, Charlotte and Elise, but even those had failed. Elise had seen past some fake horizon they had made for themselves in the stories that were never true, that James had pilfered and molded to shape themselves into better people, to shape a better future. They were wrong. James was wrong.

"It's never too late to say you're sorry," James said. He coughed. He was still alone. The daylight hadn't peeked through the gray but there wasn't much to look forward to, if anything. James wasn't a fighter. He didn't need Abe to fight for him when they were growing up; it didn't stop Abe from helping, but James would have rather not fought at all. He could take a punch and throw a punch, he just didn't want to.

"Maybe Elise was right," James said.

"I hope that's not what you're thinking," Charlotte said. The jailhouse door had closed behind her. James hadn't noticed. "They told me I could collect you. But if I show up empty handed they'll kill me and come after you."

"We can't have that," James said.

"I think we should," Charlotte said. "I think you should run." She was framed by the door, ready to run if he said "yes." They had nowhere to run to, again. It seemed to be the case with James most often now. *When the day comes to leave there is never anywhere to go.* "Let's just go. Anywhere. The island is big enough to get away."

"No it isn't," James said. "They'd find us. You don't need that. I don't need that. On top of the need to survive, how would we even do that?"

"You just give in? No hope? You won't at least try? I can't be with you if you're dead."

"So we can die in each other's arms on the other side of the island—cold, alone, and dead—wrapped up in your arms, you wrapped up in mine. How romantic. Why would I want to watch you die?"

"Instead I have to watch you."

James stood. *No matter what choice we make*

in life, there will always be a downside. He hadn't thought about the ripple effect of his life. *These are the people who I care about. These are the people who will be affected by my life and death.* Instead he thought about how he was affected. *She was my friend and she asked me for something. How long can you watch someone suffer before trying to help?* He had made a choice. The problem with choice was that most often, with the important decisions, he only got one. He should have chosen better.

Charlotte opened the gate. There weren't tears in her eyes. There weren't tears in James's eyes. James wasn't afraid of crying anymore. There were times when he told the younger kids stories that dealt with Titan tears; he tried to get people to understand that the chants of their youth in Fornland wouldn't be the same, wouldn't have the same connotations, wouldn't outcast those touched by a moment. Sometimes tearful times were overrun with fear. No matter how many times James told himself he was ready, that he agreed with Elise, that there wasn't a need to go beyond today, it didn't take away the fear.

"It's not dying I'm afraid of," James said.

"No," Charlotte said. "But *I'm* afraid of how you die."

Me too, he thought.

The air struck James's face hard as a rock, ready to be beat him senseless. He didn't wrap his face in the hood as he would have usually, because he wanted to get used to that smack on his skin, wrapped around him, turning into a goddamn popsicle. He could cry for help, except Charlotte offered him a moment of escape—hadn't he been trying to do that for years? There was no escaping it any longer. Fate had called him forward and there were two ways to turn: into or against. Was this being an adult, knowing the choices he made would always have consequences? Knowing the choices he made weren't always easy? Was this adulthood, knowing sometimes he made mistakes he could never undo and the last person he would ever explain it to would be himself? Maybe Abe would have forgiven him in time. Maybe Charlotte would have even learned to understand the reason he helped Elise, but the more James tried to justify letting her leave with the knife, the more he realized that if it had been the right decision, he wouldn't have to justify it.

There went the cell. There went the building. Outside he could see Charlotte and the Icedome in the distance. The gray seeped over the sky and bled down into the ground. The day held an overt tone of terrible that he had to sludge through along the path to the dome. The final walk he would ever make; he wished there were some sun to shine for one last minute of his life. It was a wish, not a forecast. Charlotte didn't pull up her hood either. The fringes of her hair poured over the fur of her coat and blended with the dark hair and the lengthening white tips.

"It's getting longer," James said.

"It's just a reminder," Charlotte said.

"Of the snow? I don't think you need to be reminded."

"Happier times," she said.

"They're always happy when you look back," James said.

"Not all of them," she said. "Just the ones with you."

At that moment James was glad she hadn't cut her hair; there was a second he wished she never would. Every time he looked at her hair he could think of them together before it all came to this, along the creaky bedframes of Fornland, and think how scared he had been to talk to her in the first place. How trivial it all seemed now, that fear of failure, that she might have turned him down and laughed in his face. With the snow all around him and the long, slow walk to the blank sleet of the dome, the funniest thing James could think of was all the fear that absorbed him and how none of it ever mattered then. But it had shaped his inability to do anything now.

Smoke from the volcano rose into the sky. The fumes lingered and promised to someday destroy Fornland the way the snow couldn't. It was a promise they welcomed in a way. At least James welcomed it, thinking of the volcano's warmth and all it had given them—the hot springs, the heat, the ability to cook. In the shadow of the volcano they had found life for the settlement and the island. Why couldn't he convince himself to continue, to push forward? Where was the will to live that possessed the rest of the kids, that pulsed through Abe, that once gave James the power to orate the lives they could have had—at least in their minds?

Charlotte wrapped her hand around James's. He found warmth there, beneath the smoky sky. Her skin was soft and dry. Sweat leaked from his pores. The heat stemmed from his fear, he knew, and kept his body perspiring. He kept searching for that heartbeat he knew was somewhere inside, some form of heroism that would overcome his cowardice, the part of him that gave Elise the knife, that turned away from Marcus's death, that led him into a complacent existence in a cell.

He searched the sky for wings, hoping he could see the outstretched wingspan of a bird he could identify, the grace of its flight, as if each time it flapped its wings it could push away the gray until the sun shone through. He hadn't heard or seen a bird since they first stepped foot on the island. He remembered the call with Robert, near the smoke in the sky.

They didn't see the bird's silhouette in the clouds or the trees, but they heard its loud caw as it called to another, or its children, or just a scream to prove it was alive. James had assumed the bird had been eaten by a dog, or that it had just faded away in seclusion. It may have not even have been the same bird; the source didn't matter. The sound filled James with some vague sense of hope that had been absent seconds before. Why it took a bird to prove to him that life could survive in this tundra, he didn't know—the dogs lived in the forest, the deer found a way and a life on the island, even the settlement grew. All that did was fill him with the dread that if the snow didn't get to them, the dogs would. When the bird cried into the air, a form of delicate nature, he felt that even in the wretched ruggedness of their world life could endure—the life he hoped for could endure. The bird never appeared, but the call stayed loud and crisp. He could have been hallucinating but that didn't matter now, not to him. If ever there was a time he needed a tangible thread to grip to, this was it. He didn't care how strong the thread was, all he needed and wanted was to grip it with his hands, his teeth even, and let it string him along until it brought him back home.

"Did you hear that?" James asked.

Charlotte looked at him. He looked at the sky. There was wonderment on his face, a look of a child noticing something new for the first time, the attempt to understand it, how it worked, how it came to be. He didn't need to know any of that; he just needed to hear it again.

"I didn't," Charlotte said.

Don't say that. I don't need it to be real, I just need to believe in it. He couldn't stop looking at the sky. If he looked down at Charlotte he might notice what wasn't there, what she missed in her smile, that she wore no smile, and the only thing he hoped for wasn't even in the air. They came closer to the dome. The cold started to worry him. The dome started to impose upon the sky. The search for the bird had to end. He had to look at Charlotte. This would be their last moment together and even if her face was filled with the emptiness sadness created, he'd rather let her emptiness fill his last minutes than be filled with hope he couldn't find anyway. The dome took over, its pale blue ice curved through the air and shaped what would become the last place James ever set foot.

"It wasn't supposed to be—" James said.

"I know," Charlotte said.

"It all just fell apart," James said.

"I know," Charlotte said.

"I wanted to be better," James said.

"We all did," Charlotte said.

Then the sound came—the bird. The call soaked the island with a pleasant pitch. It wasn't just him. Charlotte turned her face to the sky. She pointed. Its wings were splayed and its silhouette soared against the distant colorless sky.

"Look at the—" Charlotte said. "It's just beautiful."

James didn't look up. He kept his eyes on Charlotte. He didn't need to see the bird's shape anymore. He didn't care to watch it. Charlotte stole the look James had yearned for earlier, that wonder that kept people focusing and wanting. She hadn't looked inspired since they stood on the cruise ship and watched the Northern Lights for the first time, the night before they settled the island.

"It is," James said. "It really is."

Charlotte looked back to James.

"I'm ready," James said.

"I'm not," Charlotte said. She reached for his hand one last time. The bird twittered once more.

"You will be."

BLOODLUST
BLOOD-LOSS

ABE

"RISE AND SHINE YOU SONS OF BITCHES," ABE SAID TO NO one. He shouted once more as he walked to the Icedome, "Now's the time to be alive!"

There's no greater day for justice than today, he thought. Curious and imposing shapes kept crossing over his bedroom at night when he tried to sleep. The shapes flew across the sheets, over the space where Elise used to be. He hadn't changed the sheets yet; he smothered his face into the bed each night where her blood had smeared across the blank canvas. Where others would see dirt and disgust, he saw the empty space of Elise and wanted to absorb her somehow.

The first night, when Tic-Tac and Shia tried to

take the sheets with Elise's body, Abe had thrown them out. He pressed his face into the warm, red stains that turned the sheets pink. He sniffed and smelled the iron where her lifeless body used to be. There was a moment in the discomfort of the night where he saw the shadow of her body stretched across the space. He rolled over into the comfort of the outline her body had worn into the mattress and sucked on the sheet trying to take in the last grace of his girl, his wife, his friend—another person that left him behind in a world that only knew how to take.

When morning finally came, he put on his clothes and walked out like every other day. The red and blistered skin on his finger was now almost blackened. He kissed the gnarled digit, and touched the space where he should have carved their initials into the door. The initials should have been the first thing he carved in the ground of the settlement. Geoff would pummel James into the ground and Abe would watch all the blood rush out of James's body in an attempt to fill what was no longer there—*who* was no longer there. He twistedly hoped that when the blood left James it would fill Elise and bring her back to life. It was obvious that the more James bled out the faster Abe would lose his former best friend. Elise would still be gone. And in the end Abe would be alone.

"Wake up you glorious sons of bitches, this is your time to shine!"

In the early morning, Abe held onto the stained knife Elise had used to decorate her wrists. Tic-Tac had said no one would want to use that knife anymore anyway so it shouldn't be against the rules if Abe kept it. Shia had said that it should stand as commemoration to her life and the stories of Fornland. Abe agreed with both of them. He kept it on the nightstand next to her side of the bed, next to the stained sheets, until they could figure out a way to display it for everyone to see, always.

The Icedome was empty; the crowds had yet to arrive, and the sleek grounds were the type of immaculate white that would have glared in the sun, if there had been sunshine at all anymore. It was rare that Abe ever stood in the dome. He never liked what people did in there but it was necessary for their survival. Disputes had to be dealt with, and swiftly, otherwise they could fester. Death and destruction were the opposite of what Abe wanted but this was the best assurance of survival. They did what they had to in order to survive, and with the entire settlement wanting to survive, they had to follow the rules to do it.

Abe looked out at the covering icicles that created the grates shaping the dome. It wasn't hard to form, but it was hard to imagine such an imposing palace, a coliseum meant to house death to make sure it didn't seep out into the settlement. In here the gladiators killed and were killed. In here was chaos. Out there was civilization. Somewhere in between were the cries and chants of both.

Abe stood at the center of the dome, took the knife, and carved his and Elise's initials into the ground large enough to be noticed, large enough to stand on—grand, elegant, and there for everyone to remember the importance of her, the dome, and the settlement.

Æ

Elise was the reason James and Geoff were fighting, the reason James would die. In the guise of justice there could be vengeance. Their initials were carved, ice was cut, and blood never came off of the knife.

DON'T MAKE THEM WATCH

CHARLOTTE

CHARLOTTE COULD HEAR THE CRIES OF THE FORNLANDERS RISE up in the open gray. On her way to the greenhouse, she spotted Rudy at the door of the infirmary. Abe had ordered a padlock placed on the door. Rudy locked it and looked up at Charlotte. He pulled a forced side smile from the air and nodded. Charlotte nodded back and continued to walk. Rudy winced when he moved, still not healed from the lashes Abe had demanded.

"He doesn't get any medicine," Abe had said after the lashes.

"That's barbaric," Charlotte had said.

"It's because of him we have less than we should."

183

Claire had done all she could to ease Rudy's pain without painkillers. She packed his back with snow and tried to make ointments with whatever live leaves she could find, with a little help from Charlotte and the sprouting greenhouse. Sometimes the memory of pain was worse than the initial sting. But at least he was alive.

Rudy put his head down and walked in the opposite direction of the Icedome.

When Charlotte entered the greenhouse, Autry was already there. Charlotte dug her hands deep into the pots to try and turn the soil. She should have been at the dome, but she couldn't make herself sit there and watch the ridiculous display of shame that would leave James broken, or worse.

"You know you should be at the dome," Charlotte said. "Right?" It was illegal to miss a challenge. All the settlement had to be there, unless sick.

The rules said Charlotte needed to discipline Autry, or at least report her. Who gave a shit about the rules? Charlotte wouldn't turn in Autry and she wouldn't turn in Rudy either. That's what had brought her to the greenhouse in the first place.

"I don't like the dome," Autry said. Dirt already ran across her cheeks. Her hands were covered in dark soil. "Elise told me I didn't have to go."

"Elise isn't—" Autry ran to Charlotte and hugged her. Her head came up to Charlotte's bellybutton. Her arms couldn't reach around Charlotte. Her hands stretched and reached and left dirt prints on Charlotte's coat. She didn't mind.

"I know she isn't here anymore," Autry said. "But I can't look at the dome."

"Neither can I," Charlotte said. "I won't tell anyone if you don't."

Charlotte pulled Autry away and kneeled down to look into her eyes. "You promise?" Autry nodded.

The noise of the crowd rose and fell. Charlotte wanted to plug her ears; the screams and shouts were hard to ignore. The last thing she wanted was to know the outcome with it unlikely that James would win.

"What are you working on?" Charlotte asked

as she took her sleeve and brushed the tear streams from Autry's cheeks. Sometimes Charlotte wanted to go back to being that young, when life was black and white and it was okay to cry.

"I wanted to see the palm trees and the basil."

"How come the basil?"

"Look how big it is! And it's so green."

Other than the faded clothes and stolen pictures people had taken from the ship cabins and hung in their rooms, green wasn't a color the settlement saw often. Sometimes Charlotte would come out of the greenhouse and find kids looking through the window just to catch a glimpse of the fresh, vibrant color during their break. She couldn't imagine not remembering a color but some kids didn't have as many memories of parks and grass, if they had any memories of them at all. *Dogs used to shit on the grass.* Charlotte cracked a smile at the thought.

It used to be easy to get water without having to boil it too, when she could just turn on the faucet and potable, cold or hot, water would flow. It was easier not to think of life as she had known it. Life was ever-changing and was about to change again. Every day she lost something else, from her parents to her boyfriend, and sooner or later, her life. But what kind of life would she be living at that point?

"It has grown pretty ginormous," Charlotte said.

Another burst came from the dome.

"I don't like when they cheer," Autry said.

"Me neither," Charlotte said. She went to put her coat in the corner, a place void of plants and dirt. Autry ran to the mint and sniffed the leaves.

"I remember that smell," she said. "It was winter and that smell would be all over."

"That's peppermint," Charlotte said. She placed her coat down and looked out the window in the direction of the forest, away from the dome. A part of her felt if she looked away from the dome, the fight would go away, maybe even the cold would disappear.

"Is there a difference?"

"Well . . . to tell you the truth, I have no idea." Autry smelled the plant once more.

"It smells way better than what this place used to smell like."

"We can agree on—" Charlotte saw a figure in the distance halfway between the forest and the settlement, with four legs and a thick coat. It sniffed the air and circled the ground. It searched for something. Charlotte's heart pounded. It was the closest she had been to a feral animal if she didn't count the time at the San Diego Wild Animal Park when a giraffe dipped its head over the enclosure and took some of her popcorn with its long, black, thick tongue. She didn't count that.

She waved Autry over and helped lift her to window's height.

"What is it?"

Charlotte hushed Autry.

"Keep your voice down. We don't want to scare it away." They were far enough away that Autry's voice wouldn't carry, but Charlotte didn't want to take the chance.

The dog was alone and graceful, with a proud, wolf-like air as it ambled around the tree line.

"What is it?" Autry whispered.

"It's a dog."

"It looks like a wolf."

A rumbled roar came from the dome. The dog's ears perked and twitched. It looked at the settlement. Another roar tore through the air. Charlotte winced. Autry covered her ears. The dog leapt and ran, elegant in its long strides and powerful legs. If Charlotte could run that fast, with such focus and awareness, she might have tried to run away a long time ago. That would have meant she had somewhere to go, and everyone knew that there had never been a place to run before Abe found the ship. When she watched the dog run into the forest, its body turned into a silhouette that fell behind the darkness in the dense trees.

"The shouting scared me too," Autry said.

Charlotte nodded. It was animal instinct to survive. Animals followed their instincts—unfortunately for some people.

THE ILLICIT COMFORT
OF COLD

JAMES

THE DOME RUMBLED BENEATH JAMES'S FEET, AND SOMEWHERE between the ice on the ground and the ice in the air, he felt trapped. Etched into the ground was a carving. He couldn't see the design from where he stood but the ice shavings were scattered like lint balls over the center of the dome. He searched the crowd for Charlotte; if he saw her face it meant she would watch him die and he didn't want her to see, but if he found her now he'd know where to look when the time came. Except, now, he wasn't sure he wanted it to come at all.

The bird's caw echoed in his ears. It gave him a sound to hear over and over instead of the jolt and cries of the crowd. The settlement yearned for death. It had lost all civility; it was stripped away. The crowd had turned into something different from people. Their faces were unfamiliar to James, but he had seen that type of bloodlust before. The entire settlement turned into a bunch of scavengers, like the ones from San Diego, ready to tear everyone to bits if it meant a taste of blood. They had sampled the flavor of the sanguine fluid with drops of it on their lips. Soon they would need more than a drop, a small taste no longer good enough. They would want glasses of blood to gulp down. That glass would turn into a jug, the jug to a barrel, to a lake, to a sea, and they would never be satisfied no matter how many people they watched die, how much blood they drank. This was the world Abe and James had created—order on the outside and riled with bloodlust and inhumanity.

When James looked into the crowd he could see Abe staring down with a sick twitch at the corner of his lips, a look that said he knew more about what would happen than James did. What more could there be to the future than *James is about to die*? Twisted smile or not, it didn't change the future and it didn't change the past. The last stand would come by proxy. Geoff would do what Abe wanted but was prevented by his law from doing himself. If anyone would be the person to take James's life, it might as well be Geoff. James had never liked Geoff; what would be the point of someone else doing it?

Geoff already stood at the far end of the dome beneath Abe's smirk. Like every other defendant before him, James was stripped down before entering the dome, torn from his jacket, ripped from his pants, stripped of his socks; two large hands that he couldn't and wouldn't turn against tossed him inside. Geoff's hair was red in the light that hit the ice-bars. Sweat had already formed on his face. He had come prepared, warmed up and ready to fight. James was pushed into the circle and felt the confetti of shaved ice against his toes. He could see Geoff's muscles tensed and flexed and wiry. The nakedness

James felt came from the undeterred shroud of vulnerability.

Geoff stayed along the border of the dome. He shifted his weight from foot to foot, throwing punches into the air, left and right. James searched for Charlotte again against the greedy faces in the crowd. He found no one he wanted to see. Shia and Tic-Tac stood close to one another, one's face stoic, the other's fearful. Tic-Tac had become perseverant. If anyone had seen as much as he had seen, been through as much as he had been through, they probably would have chosen Elise's way out. Tic-Tac endured. By the look on his face no one would have guessed any of it even bothered him.

Sarah didn't stand near him. Her face was among the missing. It was illegal to miss a challenge. All the settlement had to be there, unless sick. Even James, before he was stuck in the center of the dome, was part of the mandated group of people who had to watch the clothes come off and the blood come out. Blood would leak onto the ground and cover it, becoming freshly paved with ice the next morning. That was why the ground confused James now. It wasn't fresh but carved. He stood away from the center and noticed the outline of a familiar shape, the initials that covered the sidewalk by Fornland, graced the door in the cruise ship, and was written in blood in Abe's room. Was that why he smirked? Was that what Abe thought he was fighting for?

"One thing," Abe said. He pressed his face between the bars. "The winner uses this." He dropped the knife into the dome, smeared and crusted with remnants of sanguine. "You know the rules. What are they?!"

"One winner! One life!" the crowd yelled. It made the bars shake. It made James's head rattle. The noise reverberated through the dome louder and harder than it did outside of the bars. It had started.

"You can't narrate your way out of this one," Geoff said.

James coughed. He hadn't had a chance to warm

his body against the cold. His muscles were stiff and his lungs were tight. Geoff looked limber, ready to move, run, punch, kick; he looked ready to fight. James wanted to fall to the ground and stick to it. This wasn't Fornland anymore. He didn't need to hide away from his past; he couldn't hide away even if he wanted to. He couldn't find extra space to brush his teeth to avoid his would-be killer. Geoff couldn't slam James's head into a slab of concrete. James had no reason to stop once Geoff's fist hit his face. One winner, one life. For the first time in a long time James wanted to win. He wanted to live, not out of fear but the opposite, some recent belief there was a reason to survive.

"You were never one for a plan," James said.

"Get to it," Abe said.

Geoff rushed to the knife at the center of the dome. James rushed to Geoff. Geoff tried to bend, slide, take the knife. He missed. James's knee went into Geoff's face. It was like kicking a rock. James pushed the knife away. It slid to the crater wall.

Geoff kicked James in the stomach. His breath left him. His intestines almost ran out through his mouth, hit so hard he thought he would vomit. Geoff brought James to the ground. Geoff's fists were like boulders, each hit was another smash against James's bones. James felt the blood run from his nose, his mouth, maybe his eyes. Maybe they were tears. His blood splattered on Geoff's fists, Geoff's skin, the pale ground. Where wouldn't blood go if given the chance?

James wished it were like a movie where the more the fists and kicks flew at him, the slower time moved, where he could see the light flicker and each individual breath Geoff took before it happened; James would be able to stop Geoff's rock-solid fists from connecting to his face and stomach. This, like all of James's life, was nothing like a movie. Geoff's punches kept coming and James took them. It was worse than the time he was found bloody and broken on the kitchen floor, the object of Kevin

Summers's lashings. If James could get one shot, he would have to take it.

In the shuffle, in the confusion, Geoff tried to reach for the knife. He needed to hold it in his fingers and stab James, take the life from him as *that* knife had taken the life from Elise. Then it came. It was luck, but luck was enough if James knew what to do with it. He coughed, his chest heaved, he tasted the iron in his mouth that came from the blood in his lungs. He spit it into Geoff's eyes.

James blocked Geoff's fist, who was too preoccupied with trying to grab the knife and the spit-up blood seeping into his cornea. James swung his elbow out and it connected with Geoff's nose. Another explosion of blood followed Geoff's cheeping cry and the crunch of broken cartilage. Geoff pulled his head away and fell away from James. James kneeled on top of Geoff, a position he remembered from when Kevin had beaten him those years ago: knees on the shoulders, just keep punching. He did. *Just keep punching until Geoff goes limp, until his hand stops slapping your legs, until his legs stop kicking, until the only thing you can see on his face is a smeared fountain of pouring blood that won't stop. Don't stop. Don't stop. Don't stop, don't stop, don't stop, don't stop, don't stop!*

"You know the rules!" Abe said. The voice rang down on the dome and filled the space with more than death but sacrifice. James stopped. He stood up. Geoff didn't move. James coughed. He picked up the knife and stood over Geoff. It would take one quick move—sweep down, over the throat, into the chest plate, or slit the wrists as a "fuck you" to Abe. It would take one quick motion and James would win. One winner, one life.

James dropped the knife. He looked at Abe. James didn't want to live this way.

ONE WINNER, ONE LIFE

ABE

James dropped the knife and refused to kill Geoff.

"Do it," Abe said. Abe didn't want to see Geoff die any more than he wanted to see James survive. It was the law: one winner, one life. James helped to create the law and they couldn't change it just because he didn't feel like following the rules. That was how James had gotten himself into this god-damned mess in the first place.

James sat on the ground next to Geoff. His body heaved. No one was sure if it was sweat or tears that ran down his face. It was cold but he didn't seem to notice. His feet turned blue, but it could have been the shards of ice that had littered the arena.

"No one leaves until one of you wins," Abe said.

"Then no one leaves," James said.

Abe went down into the dome. He ignored the blood splatter on the initials he had carved in the arena. He picked up the knife. The metal shimmered with old crusted blood and fresh splatter. The warmth of the handle remained, even in the cold veins pulsing through Abe's hand. He forced the knife handle into James's hand.

"Do it," Abe said. "This is how we survive."

James tried to pull his hand away. He tried to push himself against Abe but the fight had left him. His feet slid against the ground. He couldn't stand up.

"It needs to be done," Abe said. If people didn't follow this rule, what would keep them from following other rules? The accused, the criminal, who refused to kill Geoff, who let Elise die, let her steal the knife in the first place, should have been the one to die. But he had won. Geoff was incapacitated; Geoff lost fair and square according to their rules, their trial.

"This was the knife she used," Abe whispered into James's ear. His hair was soaked with sweat. Blood coated the side of his face, caked to his skin; it washed down his cheeks when he cried. "Can you feel how warm it still is?"

James pressed his face against Abe's. He couldn't protest. Abe could feel how weak James was, or how weak he had become. Geoff gurgled. The crowd stood silent over the dome.

"Please," James said. "Don't. We don't have to."

Abe wrapped his fingers around James's hand. His own veins pulsed and thumped. Both his hands forced James's hands down. This was what it took to survive. *This is why James is weak. Not because he is tired but because he can't do it.*

"Yes we do," Abe said. With one last breath, his cheek pressed against the metallic and musty stink of James's cheek, where the putrid fight lingered,

Abe pushed James's hand, knife and all, into Geoff's heart. "It's because you won that I don't help him do it to you."

Abe stood with Mo at the crack on the water. Mo worked alone, and he seemed on edge with Abe watching him work. Abe didn't care. He needed to make sure that this was done.

When had James become such a demagogue? When had they grown so far apart that the best thing for everyone was for James to be thrown into the cracked graveyard of the ocean and forgotten? His stories would live on as the basis of the settlement but James had to go—except he just wouldn't die.

"Why couldn't he have just followed the rules?" Abe asked.

"Some people think the rules aren't meant for

them," Mo said. He took a pick and began to tear away at the edges of the ice along the water.

"They're for everyone," Abe said. "That's why they're there. They protect everyone."

"Too bad *everyone* is more important than this *one*," Mo said. He pulled at Geoff's body. The crack became a hole and the water was dark beneath the ice.

Mo tugged against Geoff's body once more.

"James wouldn't," Abe said. "So I had to. That's what being a leader is."

Geoff fell into the hole.

"It'll be covered by the morning," Abe said. "You have to do whatever it takes."

"You believe that stuff?" Mo asked. Abe nodded. "Then why even bother locking James up tonight?"

"We haven't had someone defy the dome. We need time to consider the consequences."

"It would be easier if I didn't have to come and break another hole. It's never as sturdy with more than one hole in a short amount of time. Why did you come?"

"I wanted to make sure he made it."

"You don't think I do my job?" Geoff's body drifted away from the hole and disappeared beneath the ice.

"I needed to . . . "

"There's not much out here but emptiness," Mo said. "If you were searching for something more than that, you wouldn't find it here."

"What happened to your parents?" Abe asked.

"The same thing that happened to all our parents," Mo said. "They were taken away and forgotten about."

"We won't be forgotten," Abe said.

"Yes," Mo said. "We will. Like the kids beneath this ice will, like the mainland will, like all of the shit that came before us has. You can't help that. I'll tell you this: it's the one thing I can guarantee. Seeing what it's all like? I'd say it's better that way."

Mo slapped his hands together, grabbed the pick, and trailed away.

Their lives would amount to something more here than they would have in San Diego; Abe didn't need one of James's stories to believe that. They rebuilt the world in their image because they could, because they needed to. Of all the history Abe had forgotten and all the history he decided he didn't need, now more than ever, he refused to end up that way. Elise hadn't found him important enough to stay for. James hadn't found him important enough to die for. Abe dipped his thumb into the water. The frost took over the tip and wanted to spread. That was what fear felt like, the fear of being forgotten and the fear of being alone. He took out his thumb and placed his black-tipped index finger in the water. The cold touch evaporated, along with the fear. He had lost feeling and color in his finger days ago. The pigment and numbness spread.

James hadn't suffered any more than anyone

else at Fornland. Abe took his finger from the water and flicked the excess wet away. They would have to come up with a new punishment for James. Abe would have to.

He took the knife from his pocket, where the memory of Elise was now tainted with the cowardice of James and the loss of Geoff. Too much blood stuck to the blade, covering any reflection of him or a hidden image of Elise he hoped to find. The biggest part of Abe wanted to drop it into the hole and forget that it had ever existed. *You can't pick and choose what you want to hold onto.* Without the knife, he would lose the last part of Elise. She was the last part of him that tethered him to this snowy wasteland at all. He wanted to survive to show her he could, that all of Fornland could, that she could have—that she should have stayed. The handle remained warm. Layers of dried blood dulled the blade. The knife had captured Elise no more than it had captured

Abe, only a relic of what he wanted, as opposed to what was.

"You should have stayed," Abe said. He dropped the knife into the water and watched it sink, weighed down by his memories.

ALREADY
INTO THE WILD

JAMES

JAMES STILL HAD PINK AND RED STAINED OVER HIS SKIN, HIS own blood and Geoff's blood. As much as he never liked Geoff, he never wanted to see him gurgling blood or punch him to an unrecognizable mess, where his nose looked like a second mouth covered in red tape. James didn't have the energy to fight with Abe. Abe was stronger, more resolved, filled with more hate, and more energized; Abe was just *more*.

James thought he'd never be able to wash the blood away. He had too much blood on his hands, and so much of that blood wasn't his. He had seen too many bloody faces he could never forget. He had witnessed too many bodies mashed up. He had found too many girls with their wrists slit. He had watched too many people torn apart. James held onto each person in his brain like a candied apple rotting at its core. He wanted out. He had wanted to survive the dome and he had, but at what price? The bird had reminded him he wanted to survive, and Abe's ruthlessness made James question all their lives all over again—some endless cycle of horrible wonder.

The door opened. James had become too familiar with how the wind rushed through the open door and between the bars of his cell. They never gave him his clothes back. He couldn't hide from the frigid wind beneath a coat or even god-damned socks. He sat in his underwear for the past five days with blood covering his body. The guards would come in with his food and slide it beneath the bars. Sometimes they would give him a pack of snow to press against his swollen face. No one else came to visit. No one spoke to him. He wasn't sure anyone was allowed. Charlotte never showed her face at the dome. He was surprised she wasn't in a cell with him. The wind chilled his skin. Any rush of adrenaline and hope to urge him forward had vanished, letting his body freeze over. He curled into a ball and hoped the wind would fade away. He stopped praying for his clothes after the first night when Abe came in and dumped a fresh pack of snow over his bare body. James figured he wasn't going to get his clothes back after that. When the door opened this time he waited for another tray of food, another smack of snow, but he got neither.

"We should go," Charlotte said.

"I've heard that before," James said. It was never easy for him to act coy but the sense of *deja vu* was too hard to overcome. Like the bird, he wasn't sure if this moment was even real. Charlotte hadn't seen him for days and he was in and out of fever dreams since the moment they threw him back in his cell. He could make friends with the walls or the wisps of steam that came through the floor. It helped him when he curled up and tapped on the floorboards, tapping to a rhythm he thought he could remember from when they still had music and instruments.

"If I could hug you close and fast I would," James said. He thought the air was more tangible than the girl he wished stood near him, real or not. "If it's all just a dream I'll wake up somewhere next to a window where the sunshine is almost too bright."

"If only," Charlotte said. She stuffed clothes through the bars. "It's time to put these on."

James grabbed onto the clothes and sighed. The sigh turned into a cough. Every time he felt the gruffness in his lungs, it tore at the fabric of his organs. He couldn't deny it was the thing that hurt him, and that he hated, that had saved his life. He pressed the clothes to his face and breathed hard.

"You don't have time for this," Charlotte said. "We don't have time."

"We?"

"I can't let you leave without me," she said. "I can't make it that easy for you."

"What about the committee?" James said. "Sarah, Tic-Tac, the settlement?"

"There will always be another settlement."

"You don't believe that."

"No, I don't, but if we don't leave now, we won't be able to talk about it later, either."

Charlotte broke the lock and opened the cell. If it had always been that easy, why hadn't she done it earlier? Not that it mattered now; they needed to go. Charlotte helped James put on his coat. His joints ached and his body was bruised, so it took him longer than it should have to make regular movements: extend his arm, make a knuckle, flex his toes—smile.

"I'm ready," James said. "Don't I look fabulous?"

"Of course," Charlotte said. Her smile was one of content, finding peace in the tumult of their seconds, just because James could make a joke when his face looked like it had been filled with candy and busted open with a bat. *It won't get more fabulous than this.* Now was their chance to leave and it would be their only chance; James wanted to get out, with her, now and forever.

A cold and gentle breeze blew, but James felt like a feather caught in a storm. The light fell away. Charlotte led him slowly but steadily in the opposite direction of the Icedome. James didn't want to look at it but he couldn't help but stare. The ice turned a dull orange in the pale light. The faces that had crowded around the outer walls were gone but were rowdy and feral in his mind. How serene a house of death and destruction could be when you take out one component: the masters of that house that turned something beautiful into whatever ugly thing they could manipulate it into.

"We're almost there," Charlotte said.

"Where are we going?" James asked. The dome faded into the graphic white of the settlement, beyond the buildings. He couldn't see it but it would never be gone. They passed the glass walls of the greenhouse. James almost forgot how proud he was that they built it. He had wanted to gift it to Charlotte, their secret, something that gave life, where she could cultivate life. The windows faded from view. The settlement was gone. The tree line came closer. Crunched snow split beneath them. The forest of frozen trees grew before them. Howls rose in the nearing dark. "We can't go in there. Not at night. Not just the two of us. There are wild dogs in there."

"There are dogs out there," Charlotte said, pointing to the settlement. "I'd rather take my chances with those ones." She nodded to the trees.

Darkness settled over the island. The trees were in their reach. They heard shouts in the distance that rose up from the settlement like smoke from the volcano, spreading up and out. James had his arm around Charlotte. She helped guide him with each step. He could feel her push him along, edging him inch by inch. There was a soft scent to her clothes that covered up the decrepit and decaying odor of which he couldn't rid himself. He wanted to breathe her in; he just needed to keep breathing. It made him feel safe.

"We're almost there," she said.

Shouts rose from the settlement. A howl echoed from behind the trees. *We are almost there*, James thought, but he wasn't sure where "there" would take them.

"We're almost there," she said again, hopeful or exasperated.

A howl rose, echoed around the frozen trees, and dissipated into the starry night.